PENGUIN BOOKS

13 WAYS OF LOOKING AT A FAT GIRL

MONA AWAD received her MFA in fiction from Brown University. Her work has appeared in *McSweeney's*, *The Walrus*, *Joyland*, *Post Road*, *St. Petersburg Review*, and elsewhere. She is currently pursuing a Ph.D. in creative writing and English literature at the University of Denver.

13 WAYS

of

LOOKING

at a

FAT GIRL

Mona Awad

PENGUIN BOOKS

PENGUIN BOOKS
An imprint of Penguin Random House LLC
375 Hudson Street
New York, New York 10014
penguin.com

Portions of this book first appeared as the following short stories: "Your
Biggest Fan" in *Timothy McSweeney's Quarterly Concern*; "I Want Too
Much" in *Joyland*; "When We Went Against the Universe" and
"Beyond the Sea" in *The Walrus*; "The von Furstenberg and I" in *Two
Serious Ladies*; and "The Girl I Hate" in *Post Road*.

LIBRARY OF CONGRESS CATALOGING-IN-PUBLICATION DATA
Awad, Mona.
13 ways of looking at a fat girl / Mona Awad.
pages cm
ISBN 978-0-14-312848-9
I. Title. II. Title: Thirteen ways of looking at a fat girl.
PS3601.W35A62 2015
813'.6—dc23
2015011712

Printed in the United States of America

Set in Bulmer
Designed by Spring Hoteling

CONTENTS

When We Went Against the Universe .... {1}

Your Biggest Fan .... {12}

Full Body .... {22}

If That's All There Is .... {47}

The Girl I Hate .... {69}

I Want Too Much .... {88}

My Mother's Idea of Sexy .... {93}

Fit4U .... {116}

She'll Do Anything .... {124}

The von Furstenburg and I .... {148}

Caribbean Therapy .... {154}

Additionelle .... {182}

Beyond the Sea .... {189}

for Rex

There was always that shadowy twin, thin when I was fat, fat when I was thin, myself in silvery negative, with dark teeth and shining white pupils glowing in the black sunlight of that other world.

—Margaret Atwood

When We Went
Against the Universe

We went against the universe at the McDonald's on the corner of Wolfedale and Mavis. On a sunny afternoon. Mel and I hate sunny afternoons. Especially here in Misery Saga, which is what you're allowed to call Mississauga if you live there. In Misery Saga, there is nothing to do with sunny afternoons but all the things we have already done a thousand times. We've lain on our backs in the grass, listening to the same Discman, one earphone each, watching the same clouds pass. We've walked in the woodlot pretending to pretend that it is Wonderland, even though when you stand in the heart of it, you can still hear cars going by. We've eaten dry cupcakes at that dessert place down the road where all the other kids go. We don't like other kids but we go anyway, just for the bustle. We've sat behind the bleachers sharing Blizzards from Dairy Queen, the wind making our Catholic school kilts flap against our stubbly knees. Our favorite was the one with the pulverized brownies and nuts and chocolate sauce, but they don't make it anymore for some reason. So we're at the McDonald's on the corner eating McFlurries, which everyone knows aren't as good as Blizzards, even when you tell them to mix more things in.

We're bored out of our minds as usual, having exhausted every topic of conversation. There is only so much Mel and I can say about the girls we hate or the bands and books and boys we love on a scale of one to ten. There is only so much we can play of The Human Race Game, which is when we eliminate the whole human race and only put back in the people we can stand and only if we both agree. There is only so much we can talk about how we'd give it up and what we'd be wearing and with which boy and what he'd be wearing and what album might be playing in the background. We've established, for the second time today, that for Mel it would be a red velvet dress, the drummer from London After Midnight, Renaissance wear, and *Violator*. For me: a purple velvet dress, Vince Merino, a vintage suit, and *Let Love In*, but it changes.

So we decide to do the Fate Papers. The Fate Papers is Mel's name for when you tear off two small bits of paper and write *No* on one piece and *Yes* on the other. You shake the two balled-up pieces in your hands while you close your eyes and ask the universe your question. You can ask aloud or in your mind. Mel and I both prefer in your mind but sometimes, if it is an urgent matter, like now, we ask aloud. The first paper that drops is the answer. Now we are asking if Mel should call Eric to see if he likes the CD she made him of her favorite Lee Hazlewood songs. The Fate Papers already said *No*, but we're doing two out of three because that can't be right even though the Fate Papers

are never wrong. Next, we are going to ask if I should try talking
to Vince Merino again after yesterday's fiasco attempt.

The Fate Papers say *No* to Mel again, then *No* to me.

The universe is against us, which makes sense. So we get
another McFlurry and talk about how fat we are for a while. But
it doesn't matter how long we talk about it or how many times
Mel assures me she's a fucking whale beneath her clothes; I
know I'm fatter. Not by a little either. Mel has an ass, I'll give her
that, but that's all I'll give her.

If I win the fat argument then Mel will say, so what I'm way
prettier than she is, but I think face-wise we're about the same. I
haven't really grown into my nose yet or discovered the arts of
starving myself and tweezing. So I'll be honest with you. In this
story, I don't look that good, except for maybe my skin, which Mel
claims she would kill for. Also my tits. Mel says they're huge and
she assures me it's a good thing. Maybe even too much of a good
thing, she says. It's Mel who got me using the word *tits*. I have
trouble calling them anything even in my thoughts. They embarrass me and all the words for them embarrass me, but I'm trying,
for Mel's sake, to name my assets. Even with my skin and tits,
though, it's still Mel who looks better. She's got psoriasis and a
mustache she has to bleach and still. It's definitely Mel who has
any hope in hell with any of the boys we like. Which is I guess why
she claims the men at the next table were looking at her first.

I hadn't even noticed them. I was busy eating my Oreo Mc-
Flurry, hunting for the larger pieces of Oreo that sometimes get
trapped at the bottom, which I hate. It's Mel who points the men
out, saying three o'clock to me without moving her lips or making much noise. I turn and see three businessmen sitting in the

booth next to us, eating Big Macs. I assume they are businessmen because they are wearing business suits, but they could just
as easily be suit salesmen or bank tellers. At any rate, they are
men, their hands full of veins and hairs, each pair of hands gripping a bit-into Big Mac.

Mel says they are totally checking her out. I look at them
again and none of them seem to be looking at us. They don't
even seem to be looking at each other. They're looking at their
burgers or into space.

"No," Mel says. They were looking at her tits. Mel is exceed-
ingly proud of her tits. What she loves most is the mole on the
top of her left breast. She wears Wonderbras and low-cut tops to
show it off.

"I want a boob guy," she always tells me. "I wouldn't want a
butt guy because I hate my butt."

"Yeah," I say in sympathy.

"*I* hate it," she clarifies. "But *boys* love it. They always give
me compliments. Still, I wouldn't want a butt guy. He'd always
want to do it from behind."

"Yeah," I say in sympathy again. We both agree we'd never
want a leg guy.

The reason the men are looking, according to Mel, is because
she's been giving off sex vibes all day. I never know what she
means by this. My best guess is something between an animal
scent and a cosmic force. Mel always says it has to do with the
universe. What happens is the universe feels her sex vibes and
transmits them to like-minded men and women. She says these
particular men can feel her sex vibes. That's why they're looking. She's giving off enough of them for both of us. Which is why

they're looking at me too. They're totally checking us both out, she says. They checked her out first, of course. But now they're checking us both out.

I say, "Really?"

And she says, "Totally. Doesn't that make you horny?"

I hate the word *horny*. It makes me think of sweat and snorting and wiry hairs.

"I guess," I say. Though it really, really doesn't. The men aren't really attractive. I mean, they're fine, I guess. But they have these little blinky businessmen eyes and one of them even has gray hair. They look like they are around my father's age. I hardly see my father since he left, but I know he has a lot of girlfriends. Mainly women he works with at the hotel where he's a manager. I find traces of them on my infrequent visits to his apartment—feathery, complicated lingerie between his balled-up black socks, a box of tampons under the sink. And then in with his cologne bottles shaped like male torsos, I'll find a perfume that smells sickly sweet. One time one of them left a message on the machine saying she missed his body oh so much. I can't even imagine missing my father's body, and not just because he is my father. No, none of this is making me especially horny. But I say it sort of is because I know if I don't play along Mel will be angry and a pain to hang out with.

"Wouldn't it be fun," she says, "if we went up to them and propositioned them?"

"To do what?" I say.

"To, like, I don't know," she sighs. "Let us suck them off. For money. I'd say we're each worth at least fifty bucks. Maybe even a hundred."

Mel's a bit of a slut. But you can't ever call her that. She hates the word *slut* and gets pissed if anybody around her uses it. She got super pissed at our friend Katherine once, this girl at our school who wants to be a nun, because Katherine says slut about people she doesn't like and she says it, according to Mel, with a mouth full of hate. I tell Mel, What does she expect from a girl who only wants to be touched by the hand of God? Mel says it doesn't matter and really hates Katherine even though we're all friends.

Mel had to change schools, even, because they kept calling her a slut. Mostly behind her back, but sometimes even to her face, like in an eighties movie. Something about a boy she really liked who already had a girlfriend but the boy found out Mel liked him and started to like her back without breaking up with his girlfriend. So when Mel found out the boy liked her back, she gave him a blow job in the woodlot. But then his girlfriend found out about it and got everyone in the school to start calling Mel a slut whenever she walked by. I guess the boy must have felt guilty about the blow job and decided to tell his girlfriend. Or he was proud of it and just couldn't stop himself. Whatever it was, Mel couldn't take it and had to change schools. That's how I met her and we started getting bored together.

People call Mel a slut at our school too. Because of what she wears on days when we don't wear our uniforms, but also because of what she wears on regular days, which is nylon thigh highs instead of the itchy wool tights we're supposed to wear. And she rolls her kilt all the way up so you can see where the thigh highs end. My mother thinks this is why people call Mel a slut. But I don't think so. Not to sound like an old woman, but you should see girls these days. Some girls roll their kilts all the way up to their crotches. I wear mine down to my knees, but sometimes I'll roll it up just a little on the way to school. But then it always rolls back down by itself. It's fine. Later on I'm going to be really fucking beautiful. I'm going to grow into that nose and develop an eating disorder. I'll be hungry and angry all my life but I'll also have a hell of a time.

For minutes now, Mel has been seriously calculating how much we might be worth to these businessmen. She has decided that our youth and the fact that we're both virgins—in her case, only technically—makes us way more expensive than she initially thought.

"At least three hundred dollars," she finally says. "What do you think?"

"At the very, very least," I say, playing along. I try to use a voice that tells her I'm just playing along.

I look at the men more closely. Two are fine. But one of them is rather flabby and pale with little worm husk lips and a look of hunger in his eyes that his Big Mac is not filling. His whole face reminds me of the word *horny*. I know if it comes down to it, this is the one I'll get stuck with.

"But where are we going to go with these guys?" I ask.

"I'll bet one of them's got a big, black car," Mel says. "Big enough for all of us."

Mel looks out the Windex-streaked window into the parking lot. I look with her.

There are no cars like that in the parking lot.

"There's more parking in back," she says. "You go ask them."

"You go," I say. "It's your idea."

She looks at me and takes a deep breath and says, "Okay," and gets up and I say, "Wait."

"What?"

"Let's go to the bathroom first."

When we get up to go to the bathroom, Mel saunters over to the three men and says hey in what she thinks is her sexiest voice. To me, though, the only difference between it and her normal voice is that it sounds louder. In this voice, she asks them if they happen to know the time.

All three of these men are wearing wristwatches but only one of them—the fat, pale, horny one—consults his. The other two exchange a glance and keep eating.

"It's about five thirty," he says, looking up at us. And I notice that when he does, his little businessman eyes do this little dip from our faces to our chests. It's the littlest dip you can imagine. But it's all Mel can talk about when we get to the bathroom.

"Could you beee*lieeeeve* that guy? I mean, he was slobbering *all ohhh*ver us."

And I say, "Totally, I know. He totally was."

And she says, "Oh my god, Lizzie, we *have* to do this."

And I agree. We have to.

Today was Dress Down Day, which means that though we came from school, we're not wearing our uniforms. This Dress Down Day had a theme. Normally Mel and I steer clear of the themes because of how lame they usually are, but this one was The Sixties, which we guessed was cool enough. Everybody dressed up like a hippie, including me, but Mel did a cooler thing. She found this minidress with a whacked-out red and white pattern at Value Village for, like, seven bucks. So she's wearing that and her lips are covered with a silvery frost, which she is now reapplying in the mirror. Her eyelids are lined thickly on top with black liquid liner. All day she got compliments from everyone, even though we know no one except Katherine. Girls we both hate kept coming up to Mel and saying things like, Love your dress. And then Mel said, Thanks, and when the girl was out of earshot Mel finished with, Bitch. And we both laughed.

I finish putting on my lipstick and I watch Mel apply a fresh coat of eyeliner to one closed eye, and I say, "But we can't have sex with them."

Mel waves the coat of eyeliner dry with a hand.

"Oh my god," she says, "of course not. Are you crazy?"

I heave a sigh of relief. "Okay, good," I say.

"We're just going to suck them off in their car," she says. "It'll make their *whole* lives."

"All right," I say, and run my tongue over my teeth.

I pray the businessmen won't be there when we get back, but they're there. And one of them, our friend the time teller, even smiles a not unwelcoming smile. Mel takes a step toward their table; they all look up. Then just as she takes a breath and starts to open her mouth, I grab her hand and pull her back.

"What?" she hisses.

"Let's do the Fate Papers real quick," I hiss back.

Mel sighs and sits down with me back at our booth.

I watch as she lamely shuffles the crumpled bits of napkin. I close my eyes tight and ask the universe as hard as I can in my mind.

When the paper drops, I pick it up off the table and unfold it.

Yes, written with purple ink in Mel's loopy hand.

I make her do two out of three.

"Now what?" she says, as we both stare the crumpled *Yes* of the universe in the face for the second time.

By then the businessmen are getting up, clearing their trays. The horny one, though, he takes his time about it, smiling at me on the way out in a manner that I can only describe as trying for fatherly but coming off more like creepy uncle. Mel and I look at each other and make a face and fake a shudder and laugh.

Later on, Mel will climb into cars and taxis with men she barely knows while I watch from the sidewalk. She'll agree to blow a guy in the stall of a men's bathroom near Union Station for fifty dollars. She'll wear her Catholic school uniform long after she has dropped out of high school for a man from Sudbury who looks exactly like Sloth from *The Goonies*. After she drops out, I'll see her at a coffee shop on her way to a fetish bar or to meet a guy, her earphones full of increasingly obscure music, her shoulders and arms covered in welts and bruises, full of stories involving men who I'll call The Icks because their names always seem to end in ick. Rick. Vick. There will be two Nicks. She'll tell me the stories while I stare at the welts, the purply blue swirls of bruise edged with yellow like little inverted galaxies.

Much later on, in the back of a parked van, my wrists will get tied together with a pair of dirty gym socks and I'll get terrible head from a political science major who will tell me my inability to come is psychological. I'll go to a park with a man ten years older than I am, an Indian physicist. After explaining resonance to me with violent hand gestures, he'll dry-hump me between the rocks bordering the man-made creek. Years before that, in a hotel room in the next suburb, I'll go down on a man old enough to be my father—a friend of my mother's—every day after school for a week or so until this man feels so guilty he'll tell my mother and I'll never see him again. All that week, this man will pay for my taxi ride from school to the hotel. And I'll ride in it, lipstick matching my nail polish, bra matching my underwear, feeling like a girl in a movie until I get there and then when I get there, see him waving at me by the entrance, ready to pay the driver, I will not feel like that anymore. You look nice, he'll say in the elevator on the way up, if we are alone. Nice, not beautiful. Never will this man or any man call me beautiful, not for a long, long time.

"They would have totally gone for it. You know they would have," Mel says, handing me an earbud as we both rise from the booth. "Especially that one guy."

"Yeah," I say, putting the bud in my right ear.

"And the Fate Papers said *Yes*," she adds, putting the bud's twin in her left ear and pushing a button on the Discman, "Some Velvet Morning" swelling in our respective ears.

"You know what that *means*?" she says. "That means the universe *wanted* us to blow those guys."

"So what happens when you go against the universe?" I ask her, as we leave behind the golden arches and enter the suddenly ominous maw of a Misery Saga night.

"I don't know," she says, thoughtful. "I've never done it before. I guess we'll see."

As we walk to her house under black-bellied clouds we consider the question, careful to walk the same measured steps side by side so the cord won't pull too far in either direction.

Your Biggest Fan

You've just polished off a mickey of vodka, seven kamikazes, and six dirty mothers. It's getting to be around that time of night, that hour when you feel you ought to call your biggest fan. . . . Christ, what's the fat girl's name again? Liz? Liza? Eliza? Something -iza, maybe. The point is even though it's Friday night and very, very late, you know she'll be home. The fat girl is always home. Alphabetizing her fairy tale and mythology collection. Giving herself a rune reading by candlelight. Lying on her celestial bedspread, listening to a subgenre of her vampire music with closed eyes. In other words: waiting for your call. And you are right. She is ridiculously happy to hear from you, as usual—another undeniable plus about the fat girl. In this regard, she is so unlike Some People, who often hang up upon hearing your voice, or let the phone ring and ring when you know damn well they're home. Not the fat girl—she actually gasps when she learns it's you. You can even hear how her plump little mouth forms into a quivering dark red O of surprise.

"Oh my god, Rob?!" gushes the fat girl. Because she is just so excited! Because she just can't believe you called!

"Hey . . ." Is it Ellen? Elise? Something -ise. Better not risk it. "Hey, *You*!"

You say you hope you aren't calling her too late, even though you know you are not. You could never call the fat girl too late.

"Not too late, not too late!" she cries. She is just so glad to hear from you. "I was getting a little worried, actually," she admits.

It's sweet how the fat girl worries. She really cares, unlike Some People, who have told you point-blank, just tonight, that it doesn't matter to them whether you live or die.

Well, you've had a hell of a day, you tell the fat girl. A hell of a day. "Hey, mind if I come over?" you ask her, even though you already know she never minds and that, in fact, she was sort of hoping you might.

"Of course!" she says. One thing, though: Her mom's asleep, so you'll probably want to come in around the side. "Last time you forgot and woke her up, remember?"

You have a dim recollection of a very large woman in a kimono glaring at you from the open front door, while the fat girl waved at you from behind her boulder-like shoulder. "Oh, right, mother," you mumble. You look at your watch. Shouldn't she have moved out by now?

It's been a while since you paid a visit to the fat girl. It's been a while since you fishtailed your way through a dark night of the soul toward her small, split-level bungalow only to crash and burn against one of her mother's Tuscan urn planters. It's been a while since you staggered up those steps, collapsed onto the WIPE YOUR PAWS! welcome mat, made that upside-down hanging of birch twigs rattle by banging and banging your head on her front door. You haven't been to see her, in fact, since your last artistic crisis, wherein you lay on her couch all night, drinking all her mother's Cointreau and then some, while she nodded sympathetically and made you fudge.

Tonight, as you careen down her daffodil-flanked walkway, you are pleased to find things as you left them. There is the swaying yellow square of light that is her front window. There are the carefully clipped rosebushes you once retched in. There are her mother's window boxes full of fussy little purple flowers you can't help but finger, giggling. There is the fat girl filling the side doorframe, waving you away from the front entrance. She's so happy to see you that she is waving at you with both arms high above her head, cooing, "Not the front door, remember! Here! This way! Shhh!"

"Sssshhhh," you tell the fat girl, hitting your lips with two fingers.

She looks bigger than you remember, lacier than you remember, younger than you remember too, which is alarming. Are we moving backward in time or forward, you wonder, as you follow her ample crushed-velvet frame down the Escher staircase toward the living room, which is deep beneath the earth's surface yet somehow still on the ground floor. No matter. Because look, Some People can't even be bothered to throw an extra Pop-Tart into the toaster when you come over. The fat girl, on the other hand, has lit all of her vanilla-fig scented candles in anticipation of your arrival. She is burning sage and nag champa in little copper holders. She has refilled her mother's potpourri bowls with Holiday Spice. She is bent over the oven right now, hands swathed in chef-hat-shaped mittens, praying aloud that you like Banana-Rama bread.

"Luvit," you tell the fat girl, and collapse onto the rose-patterned couch, making all the Indian print cushions crackle and hiss.

How it warms your heart to watch her race to and from the kitchen, bearing plates piled with things she knows you love:

rocky road fudge bars; peanut butter and raspberry jam sandwich triangles without the crusts—you hate the crusts, the fat girl knows and remembers, unlike Some People, who do not care to know or remember.

"I would have made more," she says, "if I'd known you were coming." Next time maybe let her know just a little bit earlier? Just so she can be better prepared?

"Sure," you assure the fat girl. "Hey, you got anything to drink?" After the day you've had, you sure could use something stiff. "Hell of a day," you tell her.

"Tell me, tell me," entreats the fat girl, pouring you the last of her mother's rosé, which is the only booze of hers you didn't polish off the last time you were here.

"It's just . . . no one listens, you know?" you tell her. No one *really* listens. Especially not Some People, you say, as you take the chilled goblet from her plump, pink hand.

Now, the fat girl knows very well whom you mean by Some People. She hates Some People. In fact, even the mention of Some People makes her Betty Boop eyes go black and flinty.

"*I* listen," says the fat girl.

"You listen," you tell her. "Love how you listen," you say, giving her a wobbly smile and a wink that makes red blotches bloom all over her neck and chest.

"S'matteroffact," you tell her, reaching over and fiddling with the little red bow nestled in the black webby lace above her breasts, "s'one of the reasons I came over." You have a new set of songs you composed, and you would like the fat girl to be the first to hear them. "Furst," you assure her, holding up two fingers.

"Really?" she breathes. Oh! Oh! How you have made her night no her week no her month no her year!

How different her reaction from the reaction of Some People, who only rolled their eyes and muttered, *Here we go,* when you offered to play your new collection (tentatively titled *Novembral Musings*). Who filed their nails and frowned through whole tracks into which you had squeezed out every last bit of your soul like drips from a well-wrung rag. Your biggest fan, the fat girl—she listens. She *gets* it. She bites her lower lip in order to keep, you must assume, from crying. She lies on her back on the floor ("so I can really listen"), closes her eyes, and nods gravely along to the loops of feedback and fuzzy distortion.

"Wow," is her first word. Spoken in a fervent whisper, with eyes still closed. Wow, wow, *wow*, breathes the fat girl, pressing a hand to her red-blotched chest. And when you ask if she'd like to hear more, she does not roll her eyes and say, *Christ, there's more?* like Some People. "I'd *love* to," says the fat girl, like you even had to ask.

Epic. Primordial. Gritty. Incandescent. These are just a few of the adjectives the fat girl feeds you along with her Banana-Rama bread, her peanut butter and raspberry triangles, her rocky road. She says it's like you have Leonard Cohen's touch with lyrics coupled with Daniel Johnston's sincerity coupled with a Rimbaudian aura of tragedy yet with Nick Cave teeth. She doesn't tell you not to quit your day job, like Some People. Instead, she counsels never to give up, her gaze wet, dark, and adoring as a dog's.

You lay your head in the crushed-velvet lap of the fat girl. You tell her how it's difficult not to give up . . . when there are Some People who don't appreciate you.

"But I appreciate you," she chimes, running plump fingers softly through your thinning brown hair.

"Well, Some People don't," you tell the fat girl; she gasps, all shock and indignation.

"Well, Some People have terrible taste," she sniffs, which is what you've thought all along. It's amazing how you and the fat girl always seem to think the same thoughts at the same time. Like you share two halves of the same brain or something, you tell her. And she agrees.

"Like we're kindred spirits or something," she whispers, lowering her eyes. And then, after a moment, she looks at you again. "I wrote something," she says shyly. "For you."

She wasn't going to read it before, but she feels it might go with the creative intent of track eight. She wonders if you'd like to hear it.

"Sure," you tell her.

You do not hear the elegy of the fat girl, which she reads in a quavering voice from a journal patterned with Celtic faeries. You are too busy watching her, being transfixed. How her hands tremble, how the red blotches on her cheeks and chest bloom bigger and brighter (you make her so nervous!), how she peers shyly up at you from time to time through a curtain of dark hair, her eyes moony and bright. And you don't know what it is, if it's the dirty mothers or the vodka or the rosé or some sort of black magic, but you can't take your eyes off the fat girl; she has transformed, as she always seems to do around this time of night, into something you could almost love for an hour.

"S'great," you tell the fat girl, before she is even finished, but it shuts her up. "Yurr great," you tell her, as you brush a lock of black hair away from her flushed cheek.

Delicious, how she shivers at your touch.

"Oh," she whispers, and only hopes you won't forget her when you're famous.

"Won't," you assure her. How could you ever forget the fat

girl? She is, after all, your biggest fan by far. And no one ever forgets their biggest fan. It's just bad manners. Bad, bad, bad, you breathe into the hot, crimson ear of the shuddering fat girl.

Now all of the vanilla-fig candles have burned down to their wicks. And all the sandwich triangles and fudge bars and Banana-Rama bread slices have been eaten, washed down with the last of her love potion. And you are dancing with all three of the fat girl to the best of your B sides. You weren't going to play them at first, but she begged you to let her hear them; she pressed the fleshy palms of her hands together and begged. Well, all right, fat girl.

Your hands, possessed by the wine, or so you tell yourself, run up and down her squishy sides, from her astonishingly firm breasts to the monstrous curves of her many flanks and thighs.

"Wrotethissongbout you," you tell her, even though you are so far gone now you do not even know which song is playing, and whichever it is, you probably wrote it about Some People, their red lips and white limbs and their wiles.

Ah, but Some People, or so you feel now, do not deserve you or your music. In fact, you tell the fat girl, you are thinking of ending it with Some People.

"Really, really?" she whispers, like you have just told her this is one bow-strung puppy she can keep.

"Yup," you breathe into her warm, doughy neck, marveling at how, with one mere breath, you can make a whole fat girl tremble like a leaf.

Was it you who lowered the lights? Was it you who dragged her up the stairs and down the hall to the overly postered, Christmas-light-lit cave of her bedroom? All you know is the hammering of your own heart in the morning, the laughter of God ringing in your ears, when you wake up naked under her celestial patterned bedspread, your mouth still full of her long, dark hair.

On a sheet of her Edward Gorey stationery, you tell her you've made a terrible mistake. You don't know what you were thinking. Probably you have a drinking problem or maybe it's something to do with self-esteem—anyway, you hope she understands. Though it's a fine note, it doesn't feel like enough. So you leave her an autographed copy of *Novembral Musings* (tentatively titled), which you hastily sign, "To My Biggest Fan."

It is only as you drive home, still drunk, through the dishwater-colored dawn that you realize it was a poor choice of words. "Number One Fan," you should have put. Of course, it's too late now.

Some People is waiting at your doorstep, tapping her witch-toed boot, drumming her fingers on her narrow white hips, frowning at you through feathers of layered red hair. She takes one look at the cat hair on your clothes, breathes your Banana-Rama-and-flesh scent, and knows where you have been and what you have done.

"Pathetic," she says. "Disgusting. With her? That *child*? What is she, like, seventeen?"

Child?

She closes her eyes, shakes her head, sighs the way she does whenever you pull your guitar from its lovingly stickered case. "I can't believe you," she says at last. "I really can't."

And if your mouth weren't so full of cotton, if your throat weren't so parched from all that fat-girl wine, you would say, Neither can I. Neither can I.

A week later, the fat girl still won't take your calls. You sit alone in your basement apartment, leaving message after message—mainly drunken, but sometimes sober—waiting for her to call you right back, can't believe that she doesn't. Mistake. Surely there must've been. It's only when you see her front window abruptly darken as you tipsily turn in to her driveway one night that you understand there has been no mistake.

Three weeks after that, you're paying your first non-drunk visit to the fat girl. You don't know why. You only know you need to see her.

It's the only time you've been to see her dry—or during the day, for that matter—and the house seems different, somehow. Smaller. Not swaying. Less lethal lawn ornaments.

Standing on the doormat, you knock a gentle knock. You knock and knock until the bundle of birch twigs tumbles to the ground and still there is no answer. But you do not give up. After all, she never gave up on you. You go around back like she always asked you to. That's when you hear the sound of inexpertly strummed chords wafting out of her open window, smell nag champa burning, Banana-Rama bread freshly baked. You hunch down in the hydrangea beds and peer into her half-open window.

She's lying on the bed wearing what appears to be some sort of uniform. Jesus. A high school uniform. Lying on the bed beside her is a tall, thin, lanky man with long hair. He looks older than you are. Mangier. Less gainfully employed. He's sitting reclined on her Indian cushions, your Indian cushions, his legs crossed at the knee, torturing the strings of an acoustic guitar. The fat girl lies with her eyes closed, her hands clasped on her vast stomach like she's dead. Her hair is fanned out all around her. She's doing her nod. Her slow, grave, listening nod.

"Wow," she says, eyes still closed. "This is so epic, Samuel."

"Seriously?"

She nods slowly, her eyes still closed. "Oh yeah. Really gritty too. And so . . . what's the word I'm looking for?"

The man looks down at the fat girl like she's an oracle. "What? Like, raw or . . . ?"

"Ethereal," she says at last. "Incandescent."

"Whoa. Really? You think so?"

"I know so."

"Rad. I really don't know what I'd do without your support, Eleanor."

"Elizabeth. But most people call me Lizzie."

"Right. You *get* it."

The fat girl, your fat girl, is blushing. "Oh my god, anytime, seriously."

You watch this fucker help himself to Banana-Rama bread. He doesn't even use a napkin.

"Would you like to hear this poem I wrote?" she asks him. "I think it goes with your music pretty well." You see her reach toward her faery journal, which is sitting on the armrest of the couch, at the ready.

"Sure. But hey, can I play you some new stuff I've been tinkering with first?"

"Of course," she says. She leans back, closes her eyes once more. And the man resumes playing. Terrible broken chords that ring in your ears long after you've stumbled out of her mother's flowers and found your way home.

Full Body

We're skipping Individual and Society so China can show me how to do her smoky eyes. We should be sitting kitty-corner from one another, watching sweat stains darken Batstone's armpits as he explains to us The Difference Between Charity and Grass Roots Change. Instead, we're in the stoner girls' bathroom, the farthest stall from the door. I'm sitting on the lid of a nonworking toilet, and China's pushed the curtain of hair from my face. My eyes are closed and my head's tilted up toward her like she's the sun as she stabs onto my closed lids—clenched tight and fluttery like a wishing child's—her own personal mixture of agate, slate, and bone. There's the cigarette and pot stink of the girls' bathroom, my back pressed hard against the cold silver flush. There's China hunched over me, smelling like some musk from a Wicca shop on Queen West that isn't even open anymore.

China's like, "Relax your lids a little, Lizzie," but it's hard because this is China, and the fact of her straddling me on the toilet giving me her smoky eyes is for me a cosmic event. Two minutes ago,

I was standing outside Batstone's class, looking at her like she was on the opposite side of the world even though we've been hanging out more lately. *How do you get your eyes like that?* is something I didn't know I'd said out loud until she looked up and said, *I'll show you.*

"How's that, better?" I ask her and I'm telling my eyelids, Relax, just fucking relax. I tell them, She's giving you this, her secret to a smoky eye, her *secret.*

"Yeah, not really." She pulls her Drink Me flask from her Matrix-y coat pocket and hands it to me. I drink whatever it is and whatever it is burns and she pulls the wand away until I finish coughing.

"Look up?" she says. I look up at the cracks in the ceiling, the dark water stains, as she begins to jab at my lash line. I feel my lids quiver under each stroke and worry she's going to get pissed at me for this. Instead she goes back to telling me how this guy who's been psycho over her lately is still being psycho. His name is Warren, but we call him Alaska because China likes to name the guys who stalk her after states.

"He's still being psycho?"

"Way psycho," she says, poking at my lids with a rough-haired brush.

"Psycho how?" I ask her, my eyes leaking in their effort to relax. I'm always eager to know how. There was Utah, who kept writing her name in the condensation on the windshield of her dad's Honda whenever it rained. New Hampshire, who, when he found out that she had *Steppenwolf* tattooed down her back, sat out on her front lawn all day reading Hesse in the original German. China said by the time she noticed him shivering out there in the snow, he'd gotten frostbite on his left ear. But my favorite was Maine, the medical artist who drew corpses for a living, who kept telling her she was the perfect woman. China kept telling him she wasn't, she really wasn't, and he said she was too and so finally she said, Okay, fine, draw me since you're a medical artist. But show me every flaw, she told him. Like, be *precise*. So he drew her and when he did China said he had an erection for four hours straight because it turned out she really was the perfect woman.

But all China says this time when I ask her, "Psycho how?" is: "You know when they watch you sleep, it's like the beginning of the end."

I nod like I totally know. Like I've been there a thousand times.

"Don't move, you're fucking it up," China says, so I stop nodding. I totally freeze.

"That is psycho," I say softly.

"Yeah, I told him it was over," she says, pressing a pencil deep into the inner corner of each of my eyes, one and then the other, like I'm being anointed. China's always telling boys it's over, and that's when they go super psycho. That's the part I love most. That's what happened with Vermont. The last time she dumped him, he burned all these photos of her and left them smoking in a shoe box at her door. Not the *whole* photo, China said. Just her face. Her face in every picture. Burned out. Wow, I said. That's sort of beautiful. And she said, Beautiful? Try insane. And I said, Yeah, that too.

"What did he do when you told him it was over?"

"Cried," she says. "But what I can't believe is how *much*. It was so intense to watch, you know?"

I start to nod, but I catch myself just in time.

"It sounds intense," I say. I think of how last night Blake

cried about how he can't believe we found each other through an AOL member profile search. He cries about that most nights we talk. That and the beauty of my mind-body-spirit, which, even though I've yet to send him a full-body pic, he says he can see clearly with his third eye. I don't see him cry, of course, but I hear it through the static of his speakerphone.

"I'm seeing this guy on the Internet," I tell China now. "It's been pretty intense with him too."

"Hold still," she says.

"He really wants a full-body shot of me. He keeps asking and asking for one. Like, every night when we talk. I don't know what to tell him."

I watch her grab black liquid liner from her cosmetic bag patterned all over with pinup girls. You wouldn't believe this liner. It's blacker than black. No color is black enough for China except for this one kind she says she gets at Target that I can never find. I feel it now as a cold stabby stream across my waterline. Sharp feathery strokes like little knife swipes that make me flinch each time.

"A full-body shot's no big deal," she says.

"I guess. Just I haven't really told him about me, you know?"

"Don't move."

"Like, about my weight or anything," I add, the word *weight* falling from my mouth like a stone.

"Shut up," she says.

I shift on the toilet seat, become aware of the taped lid beneath me, the underlying funk of the bathroom, that I'm still flinching even though there is no reason to. When I open one eye, I see China has already drifted away from me and is checking herself out in one of the cracked mirrors above the overflowing sink.

"We're done?" I ask.

"Yup."

"How does it look? Does it look okay?"

"Go see," she says, gesturing toward the mirror beside her, but I don't want to go see. I want to hang on to my idea of what I look like, which is like China. Even though we only started hanging out recently, China tells me all the time that she sees me as like a sister to her and I tell her some people say we even look like sisters. "What people?" China says. I think of the woman who ripped our tickets at the Warhol exhibit. This coat check girl at Death who doesn't work there anymore. That one waitress in the old lady tearoom we sometimes go to when we skip Lit or Government. That waitress is always asking us, "Are you two sisters?" And China tells her, "No. We're not. We're definitely not." Then she looks at me and says, "You're beautiful all on your own." I smile whenever she says this, even though I feel like she's marooned me on some desert island, taking away with her the only boat. I want to tell her, I don't want to be beautiful all on my own, I don't. But I just say nothing. Sometimes I say thanks.

I stare at China from the toilet where I'm still sitting.

"Does it look bad?"

"Oh my god, here," she says, handing me a small lipstick compact of red silk patterned with dragons.

I look at the one eye I can see in her smudged little rectangular mirror. "Oh my god," I whisper.

"What?"

"It looks amazing."

"Oh, good," she says, continuing to apply lipstick with the pad of her index finger. "I actually fucked it up a lot because you wouldn't stop moving."

I move the mirror around so I can see the other eye, then the other again.

"I can't believe it." I look over at her. "Thanks so much for this. Seriously."

She shrugs, shoves the kit in her black canvas satchel covered with Wite-Out skulls. "It's nothing," she says. "Seriously, it's just eyes."

Now we're lying here in my bedroom because after the smoky eyes and the Drink Me, we didn't feel like English. We're staring up at my Bettie Page poster, the one where Bettie is all tied up in a chair wearing super-super high heels. I'm thinking about my eyes and how I'm wearing my tights as a top. China showed me how to do this. You just rip a hole in the crotch of your fishnets and stick your head through it, then you slide your arms where the legs are supposed to be. She says you can do this with any pair of tights, but it's best with fishnets because you can poke your fingers through the mesh.

With my smoky eyes and my fishnet tight top, I must say I'm feeling pretty hot, almost.

I turn to her lying on the bed beside me. "How does it look?"

"Hot," she says, frowning at a cuticle. "Go see."

"I'll wait," I say. "I'll wait till later. I don't look fat, do I?"

And China says, "Stop it," like she's genuinely pissed. She says she wishes she had my hair, what a head of it I have, so good smelling for a smoker. Also my ankles. Look at those ankles. She'd cut them off right now. My hair and my ankles. Right now. Give her a knife. China has hair like Annie Lennox's. We weren't on speaking terms when she wore it like Joey Ramone. We were never friends at Holy Trinity, but I'd see her in the halls, before she dropped out. Spiders dangling from her ears. Mel called her a poseur, said she wasn't really into the music, she just had the look. Tall and rail thin and pale as death. The kind of girl who looks like she should be walking down a dirt road in a music video, one where the sky is gray and the earth is gray and there's nothing for miles but this girl walking in a torn dress toward you, dark lips curving into a smile, her hands splayed open at her sides like Christ's. It was only after I dropped out of Holy Trinity and switched to this alternative school that we became friends. Locked eyes in Literature, which is taught by this guy who looks like Eraserhead and lets you do projects on things like just reading Hesse.

"Do you think Batstone's mad at us for skipping?" I ask her.

"He doesn't care. Anyway, I hardly ever skip these days. I need to finish and get the hell out of here." She really does. China was two years ahead of me at Holy Trinity, so she must be, like, twenty. "So long as we don't miss next week," she says.

We have a presentation on Haiti next week.

"You can't shaft me next week," she says.

"I won't." It's true, I skip a lot. There are stretches of days when I just can't bring myself to leave my room, to be seen.

She grabs a Matinée 100 from my purse. She's in no hurry to go home, she says, because she's trying to avoid Montana. She asks me to show her the trick I have of lighting a match with one hand. It's easy—you just fold it over the edge of the matchbook and press it down with your thumb just below the strike pad. But I'm happy to have something she wants me to show her.

Then she says, "So tell me about this Internet guy. What's his name?"

I tell her a bit about Blake. How I met him on AOL a few

weeks ago. How his handle is The Cosmic Dancer, which is a reference to Shiva, the Hindu deity. I don't tell her that he's forty-seven and a quadriplegic but I do tell her that he lives near L.A. and that he's a fan of Goth/industrial/dark wave and the films of Lynch and von Trier. I tell her how we talk about what movies we would be in if we could live in any movie (for me *Prospero's Books* or *Exotica*; for him *Naked* or *Nowhere*), and what would be the soundtrack for the movie of our lives, and what it would be like to live in Duras's Vietnam. I don't tell her that lately we've been talking more and more about how I'm going to be the miracle for getting him hard again. Or how he'll get stoned and tell me all about his elaborate lucid dreams of us fucking in India. Where the mere sight of me in a sari or sometimes it's just a necklace of bones and teeth gets him so hard that he gets up out of his wheelchair and just walks toward me and we fuck on a flower-strewn altar with all these little Indian women watching. I tell her again that he's been asking for a full-body shot and that I've been putting him off. But I know from past experience that I won't be able to put him off forever, that it's only a matter of time.

"Is he cute?" she asks.

I think of the pictures he sent me the other day. One before the accident and one after. I looked at them once and never again.

"He looks like Morrissey, I guess." It's not that much of a stretch. Morrissey *is* balding, sort of.

"Morrissey's not looking so good these days," she says. "So you're sending him one back?"

"I'm still trying to decide," I tell her. I show her the pictures taken thus far. The one my mother's boyfriend took of me in the forest leaning against a dead oak, gazing wistfully to the left. The one I took of myself in the bathtub full of strategically petaled water. The ones Mel took of me in the living room under my mother's print of Monet's *Water Lilies*, my upper half eclipsed by my mother's cat seated on the armrest, my lower half artfully padded with Indian cushions. "I don't understand what's wrong with any of these," Mel said after we were done. "You look beautiful in all of them."

China flips through the photos now, frowning. "You're a little blurry in these. Also you look sort of mad."

"Do I look fat though?"

"You look mad."

"How mad?"

"Like, pissed. Seriously pissed." She flicks through the pictures again. "In this one, you look scared."

She drops the photos, and flops onto her back next to me. "You know, my dad has a pretty good camera," she says.

"Really?" I turn to look at her—eyes nose lips chin so cutting and sharp, her bones in an elegant origami configuration on my bed. If she took the photo. Did my eyes. Helped me choose my clothes. She's really into art, so she probably knows all about angles. I feel a surge of something like hope.

She nods at the ceiling. "We wouldn't even have to use flash, I don't think."

We. My heart lifts. "We wouldn't?"

"What are you, an echo chamber?"

"Sorry. It's just I've really been stressing about this."

She frowns. "Why?"

"I haven't really told him about me, exactly."

She picks up the photos and starts flipping through them again. "What do you mean *about* you?"

"Well, like, my weight."

She looks at me a long time with a raised eyebrow. She hands me back the photos and rests on her back. "I'm starving. I wish we had zucchini blossoms. I'd fry the hell out of them. They're my thing right now."

"Oh," I say.

"Or Chinese. I could really go for some Chinese."

"When?" I ask her.

"When what?" she repeats.

"Should we take them? The pictures, I mean."

"Whenever," she says, yawning.

Now, I think. With my eyes like this. Except I really need to think about location. Wardrobe. "What about Saturday?"

"Saturday should work," she says, her eyes fluttering closed.

"Like, around one?"

"One," she repeats, closing her eyes definitively. I watch her until I realize she's sleeping. I do not want to be someone who watches her sleep. So I go into the living room and just sit there until I hear her rustle awake.

All evening, I avoid mirrors even though I'm dead curious. I smell like China, who boys burn pictures of, they're so mad at her for not loving them back. I'm full of Drink Me and with my eyes all smoky, I'm totally not hungry at all. I feel almost like I could be China, like I could fold all my limbs into a chair with grace, grow faint from the smell of mushrooms like she told me she did once—they had to call an ambulance and everything. I go to my room and play the CD I'm in the process of making for China until it's time to talk to The Cosmic Dancer, and then I tell him all about how I wore PVC to lit class. And I describe the outfit in every particular.

And he's like, "Man, I wish I could see that," and, "Wow, Bettie, I'll bet every boy at your college is totally in love with you."

"I don't know about that," I say. And he's like, "I do. Every time I hear you describe yourself, I get hard. I seriously do."

And even though we both know that this is anatomically impossible given his paralysis, I say that's so sweet of him.

He says he doesn't know if it's sweet, but it's true.

And then I tell him I have this friend, China, who's going to be taking my full-body pic on Saturday. Some people say we look like sisters, I tell him. Like we're doppelgängers or something. I tell him about the time she took me to Death and I tell him about the time she smacked a cigarette out of my mouth. And I tell him how today she dragged me into a bathroom stall and did my eyes all smoky like film stars from the thirties and forties. And he says, "Oh, Bettie, I wish I could see you."

And I say, "I wish you could too."

"I feel like we have this connection, you know? . . . Like, this deep, deep connection."

And I agree. We do. And he tells me how I'm going to be his miracle. How the sight of me will make him walk again, will make him so hard he'll cream his pants, and I let him go on and on like this, describing how we fuck on the Ganges River, which he says is a holy place of transformation, with the whole of the Hindu pantheon of gods watching. And I look up at the dark ceiling above me and blow smoke rings at where I know Bettie is, tied up in her PVC. I remember my eyes are all smoky. I think of China in her room surrounded by the dragons she told me she painted on the walls, being watched by boys dripping rain like Zen fountains.

"Can't you just send me a picture now?" he asks me.

I'm just about to tell him that I'm tired right now, when the door to my room opens. "Elizabeth, who are you talking to in here?"

I stare at my mother's robed silhouette in the open doorway. "No one," I say, hanging up.

"Not one of those guys from the Internet?"

I say nothing. Stare at her sex-rumpled Liz Taylor hair. Her large body robed in black silk and emanating Fendi, which she can't afford but buys anyway. There is a lot we can't afford that she buys anyway: abstract paintings, African masks that aren't even real masks.

"Who were you talking to just now?" she says.

"Rosemary," I lie.

"Rosemary," she repeats.

Even though she only met her once and very briefly when she picked me up from school, my mother likes China, who she calls by her proper name, Rosemary. Unlike Mel, who she thinks is a bad influence, and who she holds responsible for what she calls my "downward spiral." Rosemary, on the other hand, has style.

She flicks on my bedroom light. I wince and cover my eyes, wonder when she'll go back to her boyfriend, who I know is waiting for her in the bedroom, but she just stands there. Folds her arms over her chest.

"How was school?"

"Fine," I say, lowering my hand from my eyes.

"Did you *go*?"

"*Yes*." She looks right at me and I look right back without flinching or blinking. Her boyfriend took pictures of me once. For the Internet guy I was seeing before this one. Black-and-whites.

Close-ups. In woodlots. In my bedroom. In parks. I never ended up sending those and I never look at them. Just go back, I tell my mother in my mind, but she stays standing there.

"This 'school' is your last shot, Elizabeth. You know that, right?"

She's looking away now. It's fine that she took him back after the photos. I don't think she knows the whole story. Also she's lonely, I see how lonely. I see how she hasn't been with anyone since my father left when I was five. I see she's a fat, middle-aged woman with a heart condition, so how many men does she really have to choose from? Though I never told her, she knows I see, sort of. But I thought we had an unspoken agreement that in exchange for my seeing, my silence, she would not pry into my affairs.

"I know you've been depressed," she says now to the print of Audrey Hepburn that she herself nailed to my wall and which I've since covered with zombie stickers. "I'm just worried. You're not helping yourself at all. Look at you. It's like you love being miserable." Seeing me eye her huge stomach, she crosses her arms over her black silk robe.

I fold my arms and look down past my thighs at the bedspread beneath me. I never look at my body if I can help it. It's bigger, I can feel it, but I haven't stepped on the scale or looked in a full-length mirror in months.

"I don't love it," I mutter.

"What was that?"

"I said I *don't* love it."

"What the hell happened to your eyes?"

"It's just makeup."

My mother stares at me a long time before flicking off my light.
"It looks like you got punched."

Saturday arrives and she's late. But I don't let it worry me. I've already done most of the work—scouted various locations, laid out potential wardrobe choices on the bed. I figure she'll help me choose. Once she helps me choose and does my eyes it'll all work out. China will know what to do, I'm sure of it. She shows up at around seven, wearing a tank top and a Scottish kilt and a dog collar with spikes that match her spiked hair. She's got a roll of duct tape in her hand.

I'm very excited when I see the duct tape. She's taking this so seriously.

"You brought tape!"

She looks at the roll in her fist like she's surprised to see it there.

"Oh yeah. That's for me. I'm going to Death later and I have to tape my nipples 'cause this dress I'm going to wear tonight totally slides around when I dance. You know the way I dance."

I do know the way she dances. It's crazy. She just closes her eyes and spins under the mirror ball, and people have to steer clear. "Oh, yeah, for sure," I say, disappointed. "Tape is a great idea."

"So are you ready?" And she holds up the camera like she's actually about to start clicking.

"Ready?" I repeat, and I'm thinking, What about my makeup? What about wardrobe choices? Location? Light? But all I say is, "Not yet. I haven't even really decided what I'm wearing."

She looks at me dressed in my long black velvet skirt and black tee. Her look's like, I thought you were dressed.

"This? No, no." And I point to my bed, upon which I have laid out all of these possible outfits complete with shoe options. "I wanted to see which you thought first," I tell her.

She looks at them awhile. Most of them are other loose black tops and long black skirts.

"What I *thought*?"

"Which you liked. Best."

She gives them a cursory glance, shrugs. "Whatever you think."

She sits down on my bed lightly, like she should get up anytime. She begins to pick at the fringe on one of my mother's Pier 1 cushions that I took from the couch, hoping we'd be able to use it as a prop. I wish she'd look at me.

"If you want," I say, "we could hang out a bit first—maybe get Chinese?" I watch her, still fingering the cushion fringe.

"I'd rather just get started. I brought this too," she says and out of one of her army coat pockets, she pulls an eye shadow kit.

I'm overcome by this kindness. I'm about to say, Yes! Thank you, but she looks up at my eyes. "Wait, is that . . . Are you *still* wearing what I put on your eyes, like, a week ago?"

"No," I say, even though it is. "This is just my stuff," I tell her now. "I was just experimenting. Before you came."

"Oh," she says. "Well it looks good like that. You should just leave it. Unless you want me to touch it up?"

Now it feels like too much to ask.

"Oh, no, that's okay. I mean, if you think it looks good like this . . ."

She's staring at me, blinking. I realize she's waiting for me to get going. I go get changed without her help, without her consultation. It all feels like drowning.

"So where do you think I should stand?" I ask her when I come back.

"Wherever."

"I was thinking here?" I say, gesturing toward the space between my bookcases and my CD towers, beneath my print of *The Scream*.

After she gives me a very slight nod of her head, I arrange myself in my chair and crane my neck as far forward as possible while letting my hair fall in front of my face.

"How do I look?" I say, without moving my lips.

"Like Cousin Itt in mourning. Might try moving your hair out of the way. Also, smiling."

I can't tell her I don't want to broaden my cheek circumference. She wouldn't understand. Also, with the camera on me, my face stiffens. Feels paralyzed. I force my lips to curl on one side.

"How about now?"

She lowers the camera and looks at the pomegranate-scented tea light I've lit and placed on the nightstand.

"Think we're going to need more light."

"What if I lean into it more?" I crane my neck forward toward the candle flame.

"Yeah, that won't work."

"I thought you said your dad had a special camera. One that can see in the dark."

"There are no cameras like that, Lizzie." She flips a switch on the camera and then starts clicking again. This time a flash goes off. Blinding. I reel from it.

"I thought you said you wouldn't need flash," I say.

But she keeps clicking and clicking. "What?"

"I said, 'How do I look?'"

"Like I just murdered your gerbil. Relax a little." She clicks some more. Clicks and clicks. Too fast. I want to tell her to slow down. Tell me how it looks. Give me a chance to change outfits, lighting, location. Angles. We need to try different angles.

My Wonder Woman phone rings and rings.

"That him?" she asks me, jutting her chin at the phone.

"Yeah," I say out of the corner of my mouth.

"Answer if you want," she says.

"It's fine," I say. I don't really want her to hear us talk. Also, I'm afraid if she stops now she won't take any more.

"Answer," she says. "I could use a break anyway." She puts down the camera and picks up my pack of cigarettes.

When I pick my phone up and say hello, I'm aware of how my voice changes. I become the oversexed nymph who will wander the hinterlands of Calcutta with him. The one who is all sinew and braceleted bone. I hear the wistful notes, the breathy affectation I can't help. I turn away from her while I talk.

"Are you taking the pictures?" he says.

I look over at China. She's at my desk surfing the net, smoking.

"Yeah."

"Oh, okay. I didn't mean to bother you. It's just I can't wait to see them. I'm honestly getting hard just thinking about it, I swear. I'm in the middle of creaming my pants right now."

"That's nice," I whisper into the receiver.

"What did you say? How come you're talking so softly?"

"No reason. I just said, 'That's nice.'"

"You keep saying that! And I keep telling you it isn't nice. It really isn't."

"I should go."

"Wait! When will you send them to me?"

"Later today, probably. Like, tonight, I guess."

I hang up and turn around to find China still sitting at my computer. She's found one of the pics Blake sent me in my drawer.

"*This* is him?"

We both stare at the black-and-white actor's head shot of him in his wheelchair, the one he still sends out to movie and television producers. He had to quit his job as a soap opera actor after the accident, but he still gets work as an extra, sometimes even a line or two in a movie now and then. Though you can see the wheelchair handles poking out above his biker-jacketed shoulders, the pic is mainly a close-up of his face looking daytime-television intense, like when a bomb has just been dropped in a scene and the camera closes up on the actor's expression before fading into black and then commercial. But actually it's the other photo, the one China pulls up now, that I can't bear to look at. The one before the accident, before the night he got super coked up and decided to climb a forty-foot palm tree and jump. In this picture, he's standing smiling and naked beneath a waterfall somewhere in South America, wearing a pair of Reeboks, looking only a few years older than I am now. I don't know why looking at this picture embarrasses me so much. If it's his eighties hair or the Reeboks or just how at ease he seems in his sunburnt skin, an ease I've never known, so at ease he looks almost cocky. That there was a time in his life when he was happy to stand in the bright light of day and bare himself like this, his smile so wide and open, he might be laughing. And that he would send this shot to me now. I much prefer the wheelchair picture, which is more or less just his face, his expression trying for cinematic but mostly just looking broken and vacant. There's still a lingering pride in the tilt of his chin and shoulders that I don't know how to process, that is foreign to me. When he sent me the pictures, I didn't know what to say. At last I said: I like your eyes.

She stares at his photo so long I want to snatch it from her. I want to explain. Remind her that he's a Lynch fan. Remind her of the Morrissey connection. That he was a pretty big-deal soap opera star in the eighties. He even had sex with Raquel Welch once.

Finally she turns to look at me. "I guess I could go for some Chinese now."

"Oh," I say, "are we done?"

"For now," she says, like I've exhausted her.

When the Chinese arrives, I watch her spend a lot of time opening the little packets of sauce. She spends way more time doing this than eating.

"After this, maybe we should try some other things," I say.

"Like what?"

"Like some different angles. And some locations. And probably too we should try some with the light on."

"I don't know about this, Lizzie," she says.

"What?"

"This whole thing. It just seems weird."

"What about the guy who was psycho all over you? Vermont? Who burned the photos. He wasn't weird?"

"I really don't think you can compare the two."

"I guess not. I mean, mine lives far away."

"Also what is he, like, sixty?"

"Forty-seven."

"And a paraplegic?"

"Quadriplegic."

"And are you ever actually going to *meet* this guy? Are you really going to fly to fucking Irvine or wherever he lives? How is he going to pick you up from the airport? Do you even *want* this guy to fuck you? *Can* he even fuck you?"

"I—"

"I just don't see how this is going to work, like, in *reality*. He's way old. And weird. And he's got *Baywatch*-era hair. This pic situation"—she shakes her head at her egg roll—"is honestly the least of your worries."

We pick at the Chinese in awkward silence.

"I should be getting to Java. I'm meeting this guy Andrew there. He's a friend," she says. "You've got enough there, don't you? Here," she says, handing me her dad's camera. "You can hang on to this and develop them. Just bring it with you next time I see you. You're coming to class Monday, right?"

"Yeah."

"We have that presentation."

"I know."

She goes to the bathroom to duct-tape her nipples, and while she's in there, I look at the photos on the camera's LCD monitor. They're the same if not worse than the ones I had before. I look startled in most of them. Overexposed. Pissed. My makeup is terrible. I do look like I've been punched in the eyes.

She comes back into my room with her dress on up to the hips, her top half totally naked but for the duct-tape crosses.

"Do these look like X's or crosses?"

I look at her a long time.

"They look more like plus signs, I guess."

"I guess that's all right," she says. "Can you tie me up in back?" She turns to give me her back and holds out the straps of her halter.

I tie her up, gazing at the Asian characters tattooed down her back that supposedly spell out *Steppenwolf* and wonder, what if they don't spell out anything? What if she got tricked?

"You should come tonight," she says. "I could probably get you in if Alaska's at the door."

"I better not," I say. "I'm not feeling that well, actually. And I've got stuff to do later." And I hate that when I say this, she nods, nods in this way like she knows exactly what I'm going to do later. Can actually see me listening to *Little Earthquakes* on continuous loop while I tear my way through the takeout she left behind.

"Sure," she says. "If you change your mind about Death, come by. And don't forget about Monday. You can't skip, Lizzie."

"I said I wouldn't."

After she goes, I picture her walking toward the nearby café where Andrew will pick her up, doing it quickly, even on the ice. Her big feet are the only thing big about her and she just turns them into wit. *If they were any smaller, I'd fall over. Any bigger, I'd step on you.*

Meanwhile, one of her psycho stalkers will be waiting on her front lawn. Nebraska. Or maybe New York. Looking all pitiful in the snowy rain with his waterlogged copy of *Steppenwolf.* He'll wait there all night. And maybe when she gets home near dawn, she'll let him in but only if he agrees not to speak. He'll agree, of course. He'll agree to anything just to be near her. She'll lie there on her bed, surrounded by her flame-breathing dragons, arranging and rearranging her long cool limbs while she tells him about her errand. About the pictures. About Blake. She might say it's sad. He probably won't listen anyway. Won't hear China over the fact of China. Her long limbs too loud, too miraculous.

I call Mel. We haven't been hanging out as much the past few weeks. When she picks up, she's distant.

"Just thought I'd say hi," I say. "What are you up to?" In the background, I hear a swell of somber strings, a voice of immense operatic sadness wailing in the background that I don't recognize.

"Just studying," she says. Mel only had a semester's worth of credits left when she dropped out, so she's doing two semesters of night school and a summer school stint to finish. "You?"

I tell her I saw China today, and her voice cools even more perceptibly.

"You were right about her," I say.

"I told you! Honestly, I don't know what you see in her. She's . . ."

I wait for it.

"Just kind of plain, really. Boring. And she has no taste of her own! She just copies other people. She just likes whatever the people she hangs around with like. She's all over the place."

"Yeah," I say. This is an accusation that Mel aims at people all the time. I think she thinks it about me sometimes.

"Want to come over? I've got Chinese food."

She can't, she says. She has a test Monday night and work during the day, so she should probably really focus. Mel works part-time at a doughnut shop. Sometimes, I cut class and go over there, or I go in the afternoon. Mel will join me on her breaks and we'll eat. Never the doughnuts because we agree that a fat girl with a doughnut is too sad a thing. But we eat everything else. The fake crab salad. The dill pickles. The blueberry muffins. The toasted bagels with salted butter, which we dip into coffees that we take with cream and lots of Equal.

"You sure you can't, just for a little? I just made a new mix."

"You better not be making that for China."

"I'm not."

"She can't just have our music *given* to her, you know."

"I know."

"Though I guess she wouldn't even get it anyway," she sniffs.

On the other end, I hear what sounds like a lute. A Celtic drumbeat gathering force. Layered female vocals breaking into a siren-like wail.

"I mean, it's annoying enough to have to see her at clubs." I know what she means. It's hard to take, the way China looks under the lights.

After I hang up, I look around my room. At my crackly bed cushions. At my plus-size blouses and skirts rumpled on the bed. At all the old posters of Hollywood sirens my mother once nailed to my walls. I stand up on the bed. I reach out and start ripping them down—first a tiaraed Audrey Hepburn eating breakfast in dark glasses (now with zombies, thanks to me), then Jayne Mansfield sweatered and laughing, then windblown Marilyn in her infamous halter, then Marilyn when she was Norma Jean, pedal pushers and plaid tied over her sucked-in stomach. I hesitate with Bettie, because I'm the one who bought it and taped it up there, but then I reach up on my tiptoes and tear it down too.

I'm still in the midst of ripping, my fists full of crumpled glossy paper and tape, when my Wonder Woman phone starts ringing.

I'm hoping it's Mel, but I know it's him. Wanting to know if I sent them yet. Oh, he can't wait. He really can't. I imagine telling him there's something wrong with my computer. I don't know what happened. Some sort of glitch.

While the phone rings and rings, I lie on the floor, close my eyes. I do what I'm trying not to do, which is dream myself into her clothes buckle by buckle, zip by zip, and then into her skin. Until I am her limbs and her long curving back, *Steppenwolf* branded on my knobby spine. Until I am her lips and her sharply cut cheeks and her eyes clouded in their glittering gray smoke. Until I am her eyebrow arching itself at me from the opposite shore of the room. Sure, I say to this sad girl. I'll show you. The only thing I keep of myself is my hair, which fans out around me like Ophelia drowning. In the corner is a beautiful blue-haired boy whom I've let in out of the rain. I'm letting him watch me sleep. I'm so very kind.

All the way to school on Monday, I picture turning back, shafting her. Just leaving her there alone without the cued DVDs or the Peter Gabriel music or the overhead maps of Haiti we're going to point to. Drowning up there without the necessary visual aids I'm clutching in my hands. I even smoke a cigarette in the stoner washroom past the first bell, staring at my now nearly unmade eyes, my too-dark red lips in the mirror.

In class, I let China do most of the talking. That was our agreement. If I took care of the visual aids, she'd do the talking. I let her explain The Difference Between Charity and Grass Roots Change, let her go on about how in Haiti there is this organization—she can't remember which, but it isn't grassroots. And what they did was just show up and stick a well in the middle of the town. They just dropped it there, didn't even check to see if there was a water source underneath. Or was it a pump? It might have been a pump, she says.

I realize she has no idea what she's talking about.

"Was it a well or a pump?" she asks, looking at me like I would know, even though this is her story. Today, her smoky eyes don't look globbed on at all. They have that four-tiered effect, a look that takes time and skill. Apart from a shadow of gray dust in the crease of my lids, mine's gone. When I looked in the mirror earlier, I saw the girl I was before she dragged me into the farthest stall from the door and sat me down on the taped-up toilet lid.

"A well or a pump?" she prompts.

All the eyes have left her briefly and are on me, waiting. I let the question hang there in the ugly room. I let her hang there all on her own for a breath, before I open my mouth.

If That's All There Is

So one night, on a dead shift, my coworker Archibald casually tells me there are things he's been picturing doing to me of late and when I say, "Like what?" he hands me a small scrap of paper with the word *cunnilingus* written on it in red ink.

I stare at the jagged letters. All lowercase. The *cunni* written eerily straight, the *lingus* curved and veering downward like a tail. Each letter separated by a space as though they're acronyms for other words.

I look at Archibald sitting in a swivel chair beside me, his thirty-something face red from the low-grade grain whiskey he keeps in a giant coffee mug under the desk. He's looking at me like I'm not twice his size and wearing a turd-colored shirt that says MUSIC! BOOKS! VIDEO! on it and a blue apron over that that says WE HAVE IT ALL!!! He's looking at me like I'm donning what Mel wears to go dancing on fetish nights at Savage Garden, which is basically just a few strategically positioned scraps of black lace.

I tell myself, Laugh. It's a joke, obviously. But when I force a one-note laugh like a cough, Archibald doesn't laugh with me.

"I'm good at it, Lizzie," Archibald says. "Quite good. I play the harmonica semiprofessionally. Chromatic scale."

I look back down at the note. He's scribbled it on one of those torn bits of scrap paper we keep in a fishbowl at the desk so customers can scribble whatever out-of-print or obscure book they want special-ordered. A dated history of the Ottoman Empire. Herzog's walking diary from Munich to Paris. A photography book featuring extreme close-ups of female genitalia, where they don't look like genitalia at all but like sea plants.

"I'm sure an attractive girl like you has a ton of admirers," Archibald continues. "Boyfriends."

He's looking at me sideways, but I say nothing. I just look off to the left like it's too true. After all, Archibald *did* once tell me that Fergie, our obese coworker who walks with a cane due to a childhood case of polio, is deeply in lust with me. When I pointed out that Fergie is old enough to be my grandfather, he said that Roland, the little troll man who works in receiving, has a profound boner for me too. So there's that.

"You can't be serious about this," I say, shaking my head at the note.

"Why not?" he says, looking right at me. I see his expression is as eerily sober as it is when he talks about harmonica maintenance or extols the virtues of the chromatic over the diatonic scale.

Thankfully, a customer comes up. A man in a worn suit and a trench coat clutching a yellowed slip of paper fervently in his fist. On that paper will surely be a list of about ten out-of-print books on some obscure subject. This man is one of Archibald's regulars. I wait for the man to leave even though my shift has been over for seven minutes by the time they're finished, and Mel is waiting for me at the apartment to sample some new CDs. When the customer finally does leave, I say to Archibald, "Can I think about it?"

Archibald smiles at me with one side of his mouth.

"It's not a ring, Lizzie. Just consider it an open invitation."

The next day at work, I'm flirty, casual. I even have a plan, which I thought of last night and then visualized all day in Old English and Renaissance Poetry and then on my way to work. I'll thank him off-the-cuff for the note, then suggest, off-the-cuff, that we go for coffee. Just coffee. I've borrowed Mel's Celtic cross necklace, and put my mother's lace tank under my work shirt, which I've unbuttoned down to the middle of my chest. I'm liberal with the Winter Dew eau de cologne. More careful than usual in my application of Rebel blended with Lady Danger, then topped with Girl About Town gloss. I even hazard a look at myself in the subway car windows on the way to work and I don't immediately look away.

I find Archibald in the break room, sitting in the far corner on a lopsided futon by a moldering tower of Harlequins with ripped-off covers, scarfing banana bread out of a Tupperware container, looking seriously stoned.

He doesn't acknowledge me when I come in. Even when I clear my throat, he's still scarfing his bread as though in a kind of dream.

"Hey," I say. Flirty, casual.

He raises his eyebrows in vague recognition, grunts, and then keeps eating the bread.

I sit down beside him on the futon, half-facing him, and braid my hands together on my lap. It's not flirty. I feel as though we're in court or I'm his therapist. I unbraid my fingers and run a hand through my hair. Cards, you have all the cards, remember.

"So I've been thinking about your offer."

"Offer?"

I feel myself go red in patches the way I hate.

"What you wrote. On that scrap of paper yesterday?"

"Oh, right, my offer." He smiles as if recalling the lovable antics of an old friend. "And?"

"I was thinking how it was really rude of me to just brush you off like that."

"No worries."

"Anyway, I was thinking that maybe . . ."

"Yeah?"

"Well . . . you know . . ." I trail off. Janice comes in just then, this obscenely depressed woman who works in Kids. She's eyeing us now from where she sits on the broken rocking chair, frowning over her mug of cheap fennel tea.

"Maybe we could . . ." I say, lowering my voice.

"Could what?"

"You know, *meet*."

"Really?" He looks pleased. Too pleased.

"Not the note. I mean go for coffee."

Behind me, Janice snorts into her tea.

"Coffee," he repeats.

He gives me the same look he gave me last time, the long, lingering one like I'm not wearing my bookstore uniform, but something sexy, even obscure.

"How about tonight?" he says.

"Tonight?" In my head I was picturing a date in the future. At least a week to prepare. Prepare for what? I should be spur-of-the-moment. That's how you live life, isn't it? Carefree.

"I finish later than you do tonight," I say at last.

"I'll wait."

"It'll be late. I mean for coffee, though."

"So we'll have tea," Archibald says.

The cabdriver's name, according to the lit-up license on the back of the seat, is Jesus. A scentless pine tree dangles from the smudged rearview mirror, in which I can see one of Jesus's eyes, mud colored and narrowed, the brow over it thick and severely furrowed.

"He doesn't care," Archibald said in a low voice when we first got into the cab and he tried to take off my shirt. "He sees this kind of stuff all the time, trust me."

I shook my head.

"You're holding out on me, Lizzie. But that's okay. I consider myself lucky just to be here with you. Just keep driving, Jesus," he called. "We want to see more."

"Where I go?"

"Just drive us around. Turn some circles, you know? Give us the grand tour of downtown."

A few minutes later, I'm smiling pleasantly at Jesus's eye in the rearview mirror, trying to act like Archibald's head is not under my maxi skirt, between my legs, where it has been for some time now. I'm moaning quietly. Moaning so as not to be rude to Archibald, but trying to do it quietly so that I'm not being rude to the driver. The moans come out of me like hiccups. The truth is I'm too aware of Jesus, of the passing cars, the human traffic on the whooshing streets, the brightness of the city lights, to fully register what's happening between my widely parted thighs. Mostly it's as though the bottom half of me has been cut off from the top half and the top half is observing the happenings of the bottom from a curious, empirical height. This bland man is licking the crotch of my underwear, how nice. Now he has removed them. Now he is biting my thighs. Moaning quietly into my leg flesh. There are a couple of moments when the bottom and the top half fuse, when he bites one of my legs hard or I feel his moans hum against my skin, and I gasp. Then I become a whole body of actual flesh that he is actually touching, then I feel the brush of his tongue as an actual brush of an actual tongue between my actual thighs. That's when I say, I love you, the words just flying out of my mouth like brassy butterflies.

Jesus looks at me. He heard it, but maybe, hopefully, Archibald didn't.

When the meter gets to twenty dollars, I make my moaning more broken sounding, full of breaths and catches the way Mel's is when I hear her having sex with her boyfriend through the wall, and then I pretend to orgasm. It's been seven minutes or so. Mel knew a guy who could make her come in seven minutes.

Archibald lifts his head up from under my skirt, still between my legs.

"You came?"

I look at his face framed between my knees. Floating there weirdly in the dark. His lips are glossy, his thinning red hair in disarray. He takes his glasses off and his eyes are a different color—darker, greener, with bits of yellow in them, which are probably reflections from the lights outside.

I nod.

"You're lying."

"No, I really did."

"It's okay." He pats my knee and sits back up on the seat beside me. "I'll make you next time. Oh, hey, turn this up! Jesus, turn it up. Way up!" He thumps the back of the cabbie's seat until the man obliges.

"I love this song," Archibald says to me, leaning his head against the backseat. "Peggy Lee. 'Is That All There Is.' You heard it before?"

"No. I like it though," I say. I don't. It sounds too old-timey. That cheesy swell of strings. The elephantine trumpets. The woman's world-weary voice sounding deep and dark as a well, but with one eyebrow raised, one side of her painted lips curled in a perverse smirk.

"It sounds like the circus," I say.

"If that's all there is, break out the booze and have a ball," Archibald says; he's looking at me intently but blearily. He's got a big bottle of L'Ambiance he just took a swig from. He holds it out to me, but I shake my head. "I can't believe you let me do that to you just now."

"It was fun. I mean, I don't see how it was fun for you."

"Oh it was. It's all I've wanted to do to you since I first saw you."

"Really?"

"I have other fantasies too. Lots of them."

"You do?"

"Sure. I'm grateful, you know. I'm grateful to you. Look at you. Look at me. I'm unworthy. It's okay. I *know* I am. I've accepted it. The fact that you let me do this?" He shakes his head. "I'm shocked, honestly. But I'm not going to question it. I'll take what I can get. It's like this song. If that's all there is, break out the booze and have a ball, you know?" He takes a sip of his wine jug.

"Sorry we had to do it here, though. In front of Jesus. Guess I couldn't wait. I was excited."

"That's okay. Maybe we can do it again sometime."

"Anytime. Anytime you want, you just call. I hope you do." He takes my hand, smiles at me a little sadly. "Do you mind if I bum one of your cigarettes?"

When I come home and tell Mel what happened she says, "Sounds like it was a bust."

"Totally," I say.

But then I call him the next night and he comes over.

He starts coming over regularly. Nights we work together. Nights we don't. After a few weeks, I start calling him my boyfriend sort of, adding the *sort of* only when I'm talking to Mel. We have sex that I tell myself is good, it is good surely, certainly it is okay, it is definitely not terrible, and then afterward he tries to educate me about the jazz harmonica, which he says is the most underappreciated of instruments. He'll be deeply stoned on the generous joint he rolled himself from the bag of pot I keep for him in my freezer, drunk on the alcohol he toted over here in a worn plastic bag. I'll watch him pace my bedroom, going on about dissonance and scales, his head too big for his body, his glasses too big for his face. I remind myself that these lectures, delivered in his underwear with an earnestness that I tell myself is charming, are better than watching him laugh through a very sad and disturbing film, his second-favorite post-sex activity. I remind myself that I didn't need to call him tonight, though I just did. Just like I called him on Wednesday. And Sunday and Monday. For fun.

After eight or so weeks of dating him, I still can't explain his appeal to Mel, who often ushers me into the kitchen to have short hissing conversations about how he's lame. It's a descent to sleep with him. A Descent. When I tell her casually that Archibald's coming over tonight, she says, "He is?"

"Yeah. Why?"

"Nothing. You've just been seeing him a lot."

"Just for fun, though. He likes me," I say, sort of wanton. When she says nothing, I ask, "Do you think he likes me?"

"Do you like *him*?"

"I like the way he touches me a lot," I say, thinking of how on the subway the other day, he grabbed my boob through my shirt and how it was actually pretty embarrassing and I told him repeatedly, People are watching, because they were and he said, Let them. But this is not a good example. I think of how I can wear a bra and underwear around him and I don't have to hide my middle with my hands the way I did with Kurt, a friend I lost my technical virginity to a summer ago. He was a virgin too. What we did in the half dark of his dad's truck was a platonic arrangement, so that we would no longer be freaks to ourselves or the world. The next day, he took me to see *Rent* and we had a seafood dinner on King Street. Archibald doesn't take me to dinner, but I can be naked in front of him. Under bright lights. In full daylight. Actually naked. Breasts. Thighs. Stomach laid bare. This is a sight that excites him. And when I catch a glimpse of myself in the mirror in the half dark of the hallway on the way to the bathroom or kitchen, I don't look away. I stay there. I look at my body and I am fascinated by what I now see to be its appeal. But I could never explain that, even to her.

"He touches me like . . ." I lower my voice. ". . . like he likes my body. Like, actually likes it."

"So long as you know what you're doing," Mel says.

I tell her I do. So I keep calling him. So I call him almost every night. Most nights he comes.

He's on his way right now. Probably still on the subway, though maybe, hopefully, already on the bus. I look at my watch. Running late. Sometimes the buses take time. He might have missed his connection, which he often does. Soon he'll be here. Ringing the doorbell. Running his hands down my hips. Telling me he can't believe a girl like me is even interested in a guy like him. And I'll smile like it's all too true.

The phone rings just then. I think it's Archibald so I just say, "Where are you?"

"Is Archibald there?" It's a woman's voice, pointy and full of purpose.

"No, he isn't."

"Is this *Lizzie*?" the voice asks. She says the word *Lizzie* like it's a loaded thing, a cup she's ready to smash against a wall.

"Yes. Who's this?"

Crackly silence. A dog yipping in the background she attempts to shush. The dog keeps yipping. She shushes him again. This time more violently.

Then: "Are you sleeping with him?"

Now it's my turn not to say anything. The phone feels heavy and slick in my hand. Mel's mouthing at me, Who is it?

"Who is this?" I ask.

"This is Britta," says the voice, gathering gravity. "His girl-friend."

Mel raises an eyebrow at me. "Girlfriend," she repeats.

The woman on the other end of the line acquires flesh, a face, blond hair, tapping nails. I say nothing.

"Is he on his way over there? He's on his way isn't he? Hello? Hello?"

"Helloooo?" Archibald calls from the doorway. "Anybody home? Sorry I'm late. Oh, you're on the phone," he mouths, then shuffles into my room.

I come into my room to find Archibald lying on my bed playing his harmonica, kicking his feet against my dark blue wall. A grown man in a windbreaker. Hair going gray at the veiny temples. Pants too short for his thin, white legs. I'm wearing a lace slip in which I now I feel naked, fat, stupid. I put my housecoat on over it to gain some dignity. I sit in my desk chair, wait for him to notice that I'm not joining him on the bed.

At last he stops playing and turns to me. "What?"

"A woman named Britta just phoned. She says you're sleeping with her. Are you?"

He doesn't answer.

"I was descending to sleep with you, you know. I was *descending*! And you cheat on me? And you're smiling? What the hell is wrong with you?"

"Nothing. Just you're super hot when you're pissed is all," he says, biting on his grin.

I start to cry.

Now he's on his knees explaining. He explains for a long time, while I smoke one cigarette after another. Britta isn't really his girlfriend. Not really, he says.

"She's just this crazy woman who lived on the fifth floor of our house for a while. I actually felt sorry for her, you know? All by herself on the fifth floor. She had this little dog she washed every night. You wouldn't believe it," he said. I thought of the dog I heard yipping in the background. "When I told her it was over, she started stalking me. Like seriously stalking. Wouldn't leave me alone. I guess she likes what I can do or something. But she was clinging to me. It was embarrassing, you know?"

I think of that pointy voice on the phone, swerving from hysteria to gravitas.

I light another cigarette and notice my hands are shaking.

He takes them in his. I snatch them away from him but he takes them again and this time, I let him.

"But you," Archibald says. "You are the one I always wanted. I never even thought I could get someone like you, you know? And I hate to think I've ruined my chances here."

He starts to kiss my hands. Kisses them all over, multiple times. Someone like me. I am the one he has always wanted. Never thought he could get. I feel my eyes well up again. The room becomes warped and swimmy. Then he kisses my thighs, starts to gently pry them apart with his hands. Get out. Get out right now. The words rise in my throat like bile, but they don't come out. Instead, I just sit there limp, letting him.

I promise Mel I'll end it. I promise myself I'll end it. Every time I go over to his place or he comes over to mine, every time I hear the plaintive wail of his approaching harmonica, I think, End it. I tell myself this for weeks. Fucking end it. Speak the words. But what comes out is, Hey. I missed you. How come you're late? For the first few weeks, I even picture myself walking away from him. Chin tilted high. Already lighter for having left him.

Instead I stay in bed, ignoring the nearly constant ringing

telephone from an unknown number, waiting for him to come over. Get dizzy spells whenever I leave the apartment. Start skipping class. Calling in sick to work. Panic attacks, the doctor says, and prescribes pills which Archibald and I take together, lying in my bedroom or his, the lights dimmed.

"I'm dying," I tell him quietly on our six-month anniversary.

"Oh, Dizzy Lizzy," he says, grabbing my breast.

"I love you." I say it more often, more fervently than before, the words slipping from my mouth before I can catch them, reel them back in.

"And I love you," he says, stroking my thigh. When he touches me now, I feel revulsion and gratitude at the same time.

We have sex and I cry through the whole thing.

"Hey," he says. "You okay?"

"I'm hungry," I say.

Chinese food in bed, Take Out Dinner 2B with extra spring rolls. Pizza with wings. Sometimes I'll stumble into the kitchen and make us something obscene, which we'll devour, stoned, while watching one of his freak movies, for which I've now developed a newfound fascination: *The Elephant Man* or *The Hunchback of Notre Dame* or this carnival documentary he loves that takes a cold hard look at the mutant humanity behind sideshow acts. Or we listen to jazz, also my suggestion. I'll lie there in my slip, let him go on and on about dissonance. It isn't charming or funny anymore. It just is.

I no longer look at myself in the mirror on the way to the bathroom or the kitchen. I lie in my slip, never naked in front of him now, and I watch him, oblivious to my existence, playing the harmonica, for which I have now acquired a dull loathing, filling my room with its terrible, earsplitting whine. I watch him smoke my cigarettes, his thin freckled chest with its odd hair tufts, exhaling and inhaling. *It's over* forever on the tip of my tongue, but when he sits up from my bed to say, Well, I should probably get going, I stare at his severely stooped knobby back, his shoulders hunched up around his ears, and when I open my mouth what I say is, Can I come with you?

From where I lie on his bed, I watch Archibald stumble, half-naked, toward the record player on the opposite end of his basement apartment, a single low-ceilinged room lit by chili pepper lights he told me he stole from a Mexican restaurant. I don't know how long I've been in his basement, lying on his shitty green bed, stoned and naked and full of salt. Days? A week, maybe? There are Chinese takeout boxes all over the bed and table. Schoolbooks I brought with me but haven't opened. I have no idea what time it is and I haven't been to class or work in days. We're playing the Peggy Lee album, the song "Is That All There Is?" by my own request for the ninth or ninetieth time. From a great distance, I hear Archibald ask me, "Are you okay?"

"I see why you love this song. It's great."

And I do see. In fact, when I hear Peggy Lee's voice fill his dark, ugly, low-ceilinged room festooned with its blinking red lights, the fog clears. I well up, float, am buoyed by the circus sounds, the trumpets.

Like every time I came over, I came over intending to end it. Twice I opened my mouth to say it. Twice what came out was, Let's order Chinese.

Now I'm just lying here spinning, my mouth open and parched from MSG, too stoned to move, watching two of him walk back toward me.

I don't know when the knocking starts. Is it distinct from the music? Or maybe the music has a door? The song has a door someone is pounding on with their first? Weird I didn't hear that before.

"Is that someone knocking on your door?" I ask.

"Ling can get it." Ling is one of his five million housemates. But the knocking keeps going.

"I don't see why I have to answer," Archibald says, talking to the air around him like it's accusing him. "It's one in the morning."

The knocking continues, acquires bass.

"You sure you shouldn't get that?" I slur.

Archibald stands up and makes his way toward the sliding doors. I hear him trudge slowly up the stairs. "Is That All There Is?" is still playing on repeat. Over and over again, Peggy Lee getting existential about the circus, about a fire, about love and then death. How many times have I heard this song? I continue my upward drift to the cracked popcorn ceiling, in a swaying motion, hearing voices, hushed and hissing, then louder, closer. In the song? No. Upstairs, it sounds like. I should get up, see, but my limbs are lead.

Suddenly a woman is marching toward me. Archibald pulls her back but she shakes him off, she won't be stopped. She is a giant woman out of the circus, out of my nightmares of the circus. But she's familiar. One of our customers, in fact. One of Archibald's. She came into the store recently and asked me for a book about dachshund care. Didn't have the title. Insisted I search by subject. Nodded absently while I read off listings. A huge woman with bubble-flipped dirty blond hair. She had with her then, as she does now, a little yipping dachshund on an absurdly short leash. The moment I see her I know she is the woman who called me. This is the dog that was barking in the background.

I lie there, still unable to move, while she seats herself in Archibald's chair beside the bed, the one with the huge burn stain on the seat, with the overflowing ashtray on the armrest—full of all my ash and cigarette butts imprinted with Girl About Town gloss. She takes the dog in her arms and he wriggles there like a demon-possessed sausage, yipping like mad. He's wearing a little tweed coat that looks like a cape.

I look around for Archibald but he is now nowhere to be seen.

"You're Lizzie." When she says my name, it isn't a cup anymore. It's shards on the floor.

"Yes. You're Britta."

"I just want you to know," she says, "he's been sleeping with me this whole time. After he sees you, he comes and sees me. He was supposed to see me tonight. Then he canceled on me last minute." Her voice is grave but full of dangerous swerves and wavers, like it's a car about to veer off the road.

I look at her. Her tight black slacks covered in little dog hairs. One of those awful Addition Elle sweaters my mother and I would never buy. The ones they sell at the back of the store with all the lame bells and whistles that no self-respecting fat woman would ever purchase. Sweaters for the women who have given up on style. Sweaters for the women who just want their flesh to be covered.

"Okay," I say. My limbs are lead. My heart feels like it's going to burst out of my chest, grow feet, and run out of the room.

"Ladies. Whoa. Look, everyone just be cool, okay? We'll sit down and we'll work this out," Archibald says. He's standing in a corner of the room, attempting to look grave, but I can tell that once more he's trying not to smile. The perverse grin that appeared when

I first confronted him about Britta is once again sliding around underneath his concerned expression, just under his twitching lips.

"Oh, I'm very cool," Britta says, rocking a little in his burned chair. The whites of her eyes are all pink. She's been crying, that's obvious. I think of the squidgy banana bread I saw him scarf in the break room. The Tupperware containers I've sometimes seen on his fridge shelf beside his staple industrial-size jar of Jif peanut butter, full of mayonnaisey-looking slaw, broccoli salad. When I first saw them on his shelf, I thought, How strange. I could never in a million years picture this man finely slicing broccoli florets, chopping bacon into bits, then mixing them carefully with Craisins and grated cheddar and mayonnaise. Could never in a million years picture him removing a loaf of bread from the oven. That was all the handiwork of this tenuously dry-eyed woman, who's clearly been crying over Archibald all day and will no doubt cry again. When his pager was buzzing earlier, that was her, wondering where in the hell he was. Probably she made him dinner. I picture a table for two set carefully, a sad flower in a lame vase between the gleaming plates. Some terrible bottle of wine he'd drink in two swallows. Maybe she was wearing something nice. Or maybe *this* is her something nice. Maybe she lit candles for him. Maybe they're still burning. Maybe her whole living room is on fire now.

"I don't owe this woman anything anyway," she's saying now, presumably in response to something Archibald just said. "I don't owe her a damn thing. In fact, if anything she should thank me. She should be fucking thanking me."

"She's right," I say. "I should be. Thank you."

I manage to rise up from the bed while they continue a discussion that falls in and out of my hearing.

My boots. I just need to find my boots. There's that song about boots and walking that my mother loves, that I used to sing. Sung by another woman. Not Peggy but of that era. She was poised. She was thin. She was freedom dancing in high-heeled white boots. Stomp stomp stomp. That's all I have to do through the white snow. Stomp stomp stomp. And not look back.

I get up and get into my combat boots, which I don't lace. I pull my cardigan on over my mother's slip.

I stumble my way toward the door, but it isn't easy with the drugs, my heart thumping in my chest, the air around me like invisible water, like I'm at the bottom of a lake, feet sinking in tangly weeds, pawing my way forward.

I fall twice on my way up the basement stairs and then stumble out the front door. Now I'm outside in the gently falling snow walking toward where I think, hope, the bus stop is. He's calling my name but I keep walking, trying to quicken my pace without slipping.

I just need to keep that song in my head about boots being made for walking and that's just what they'll do and I'll be safe. The road is sheer ice and I slip a little as I walk.

I can hear his voice getting closer, but I keep walking, slipping, until I feel him touch my shoulder. I turn around and he is in the snow on his knees. He looks up at me.

He is going to make a speech. He is opening his mouth to say God knows what. More about how he can't let me go, but he'll understand if I never want to see him again. More about how unworthy he is of me. More about how insane Britta is. More about how I am the one he really wants.

"Lizzie," he says, hugging my knees, and I am trying to pry myself loose.

"Asshole!" Britta screams.

I turn and see her charging toward us in the not-too-distant distance, waving a harmonica in the air like a gun. She hurls it and her aim is remarkable. It hits him right in the face. In the mouth.

For what feels like minutes, we both just stand there. Watch the blood gush beautifully, hideously out of his mouth while he burbles, presumably in shock. Eyes blinking. Then she runs over to him. Takes off her terrible cardigan. Underneath, she's wearing one of those basic scoop-neck tops I have a dozen of at home. She stoppers his mouth with the sweater. Wraps him in her ridiculous scarf. Now she's saying sorry, I'm so sorry. I'm watching the scene like it's a still. Then I realize she's looking at me. "Can you call a taxi?" she says, handing me her phone.

In the hospital waiting room we sit side by side with one empty chair between us for our purses. Archibald is semi-passed out on a gurney nearby. Every now and then we hear him mumble for his harmonica through a mouthful of gauze. From the look of the emergency room, lots of people have been shot and stabbed tonight. Lots of deep cuts and chest pains. Lots of sick babies. Getting hit in the mouth with a harmonica—even a chromatic one—is way down on the list of the doctor's priorities. The nurse told us it would be a while.

Britta is pretending to flip through dated magazines. I'm staring at the TV.

"You can go, you know," she says. "Really. I'm the one that hit him. Besides, I think it'll be a while."

"No, it's okay," I say, like my staying is some sort of sacrifice, like we're in this together. But actually in my haste to go, I left my wallet in his apartment. Not to mention my keys, my clothes. I'm wearing nothing but the unlaced boots I wedged my feet in when I staggered out the door, my mother's red night slip stained with Chinese food, and a cardigan splattered with Archibald's mouth blood. I can't bring myself to borrow money from Britta and I'm at least an hour's walk from our apartment. I called Mel a couple of times on the hospital courtesy phone. No answer, no call back, even though I left messages. Maybe she's out dancing. Or maybe she feels these are my just deserts.

I watch the silent TV on the wall above the sick people and the ugly leather chairs. On the screen, two fat girls in stretch pants are screaming and strangling each other on a stage strewn with overturned chairs. They're going to kill each other, from the look of it, until two big bald men in black polo shirts suddenly appear to separate them. Along the bottom of the screen is a caption that reads, "I Cheated on You with Your Best Friend!"

I turn to Britta but she's pointedly flipping through an old copy of *Woman's World*. Feigning interest in yarn art. The scarf she used to mop up Archibald's blood is sticking out of her large purse. It's a nice purse. The sort my mother would buy. I remind myself that Britta is another country, another sort of terrain, strange and distant from me. That she is bigger than I am. Older. Sadder. More beyond saving. That body-wise, spirit-wise, I'm just a room compared to her sad house.

"Did Archibald ever play you that Peggy Lee song, 'Is That All There Is?'" I ask her.

For a while she says nothing, just frowns into her magazine at a photo of a wreath made out of dark green pipe cleaners.

"Archibald played a lot of songs," she says at last.

I look back at the TV.

One of the fat girls has now broken loose from security and has the other girl in a headlock. Behind them, between their abandoned, overturned chairs, a thin, ferrety-looking man sits serenely. This man watches as security separates the fat girls once more. He watches them claw and kick the air helplessly. He watches and he smiles, like such violence and misery are the stuff of life. When he suddenly smiles wide, maybe at something one of the fat girls screams, he reveals a missing incisor. I think of the way Archibald looked after he got hit. How after the shock wore off, he started laughing. Laughed in the taxi all the way to the hospital, the bandage that Britta had loosely shoved in his mouth already soaked through with blood, his laughter making the blood drip hotly down his chin.

"He never played you that song and talked to you about it? About his philosophy?" I ask Britta again. I'm looking at her, but she won't look at me.

"I really don't want to talk about this with you. If that's okay."

"Okay." I look at her. I see her chins are tilted upward, quivering. "Your book came in, by the way."

"What book?" she snaps.

"*How to Care for Your Dachshund.* You ordered it from me."

"Oh," she says, as if she only distantly remembers. "Right."

"It's ready for you at the desk. Whenever you want it."

I watch these laughably obese girls lunge for each other and get pulled apart once more. Their fat arms still reaching out to throttle each other.

Britta stands up suddenly.

"I'm going to get myself something from the cafeteria." She hesitates, then looks down at me. "You want anything?"

Food. I forgot all about it even though I haven't eaten in hours. The minute she offers, I feel how my stomach is empty, that I'm starving.

"No thanks," I say, shaking my head. "I'm not hungry right now. Maybe later."

I watch her hunched, doomed shape turn away and lumber all the way down to the end of the hospital corridor, then disappear through the swinging doors.

The Girl I Hate

So I'm eating scones with the girl I hate. The scones are her idea. She says eating one of them is like getting fucked. Not vanilla-style either, the kind with whips. She's eating the scones and I'm watching, sipping black tea with milk but no sugar. Actually, she hasn't quite started yet. She's still spreading clotted cream on each half of the split scone, then homemade jam on top of that. As she does this, she warns me she might make groaning noises. Just so, you know, I know. That's fine, I shrug, feeling little bits of me catch fire. I've got the teacup in my hand, my finger crooked in the little handle that's too small for it, so the circulation's getting cut off. I watch her bite into the scone with her little bunny teeth. I watch gobs of clotted cream catch in either corner of her lips. She tilts her head back, closes her eyes, starts to make what must be the groaning noises. I pour myself more tea and cup it in both hands like it's warming them even though it's gone cold. Then I pretend to look out the window at the dismal view of the street. I say, "Busy in the office this morning," and try not to think *Cunt*.

She is, after all, a friend and colleague.

"What?" she says, her mouth full of scone. She hasn't heard me because of her groans.

I repeat that it was busy in the office this morning, loudly, over-enunciating, then I do think *Cunt*.

"Mm," she says. But she's too high on scone to really carry on a conversation. She's so high, she's swinging her stick legs back and forth underneath her seat like a child and doing this side-to-side dance with her head like the one she did when she ate the fried pork chop in front of me at Typhoon a few weeks ago.

There's her groaning and there's her stick legs and there's her aggressively jutting clavicles. There's the Cookie Monster impression she does after she describes food she loves (*Om-Nom-Nom!*). There's how the largeness of the scone seems only to emphasize her impossible smallness. Mainly, there's the fact that she exists at all.

There's also her outfits, which she buys from vintage shops, and which are usually a cross between quirky and whorish. Today, she's wearing this spandex playsuit like something out of a Goldfrapp video, which she's paired with sheer tights that have a back seam of little black hearts. Over that she's wearing a red bell coat like the ones little girls wear when they ice skate in picture books. I had a coat like this when I was five but in pink. There's a picture of me in the coat, holding my father's hand in a frozen-over parking lot somewhere in Misery Saga. This was just before he left. In the picture, he's looking down at this small thing holding his hand as if he can't believe how small this thing—me—is. In the picture, I'm about the same size as the girl I hate is now.

She catches me looking at her and she says, "What?" and I say, "Nothing."

She looks at my cup of cold tea and at my lack of scone. "How come you didn't get one? Aren't you hungry?"

"I'm going to have a salad later," I tell her.

I'm already picturing it: me in the blissfully empty break room, my Tupperware forest of spring greens, the dated copy of *Hello!* I'll pretend to read if anyone comes in. I won't turn on the lights.

She shrugs, takes another bite of scone. Then she sort of squints at me.

"You're very salady," she says.

"Am I?"

After she's done, she sinks back in her chair, pats her nonexistent stomach through her playsuit, and says she's feeling sleepy. She sighs, faux-pouts.

"Wish we didn't have to go back to work."

"Yeah," I say, signaling for the check and grabbing my purse from the back of the chair. She reaches over and pats the fuzzy leopard-print purse like it's a pet of hers.

"Pretty," she says.

On the walk back to the office, we discuss our worst temp jobs. Like me, she also left college with a useless degree in the humanities about a year ago, and since then she's had a string of them. Her worst one, she says, was the one before this one. The boss kept trying to fuck her. Also they had this photocopier she's pretty sure was possessed by Satan. Also it wasn't near any good lunch places.

"What about you?"

"The one before this one," I tell her. Actually, it's this one.

"Satanic photocopier?" she offers.

"Fax," I say, looking at the long white line of her neck, offset by a cheap black choker.

"Ooh," she says. "Worse."

When we reach the office, before we head to our respective cubicles, she turns to me, her lips and cheeks still flushed from scone, and says, "Text me later, okay?"

"Okay," I say. Then she trots off, and I see how her little heart seams are perfectly aligned down both calves.

All afternoon I have the waking dream where she gets so fat on scones, she explodes.

At home, I eat the other half of my salad with the other half of the honey Dijon dressing it came with. I make sure to draw the curtains first. I didn't used to, but then I caught the owner of the Turkish restaurant next door staring at me from his upstairs window, smoking, just as I had finished my post-salad ritual of dragging my finger pads over and over again across the empty plate and sucking the oil off them one by one. It used to be he would say hello when I walked past him in the street. Now he looks at me like he's familiar with the details of my most unfortunate pair of underwear. Has fingered the fraying scalloped edge. Waggled the limp pink bow. Held the MADE IN CAMBODIA tag between his teeth.

Post-salad, I try on the French Connection bodycon, followed by the Bettie Page pencil skirt and the Stop Staring! halter. In all cases, I'm no closer to my goal but I'm also no further from it, which is no news at all. Twenty-five days. That's how long I have left before I fly out to visit Tom, my boyfriend of sorts. Two weeks ago, when he pushed me to pick a date for a visit, I picked one in what I thought at the time was the distant future so that I could be closer, much closer than I was when he saw me last time. But then I remind myself that it's been fifty-seven days since he last saw me, since I waved good-bye to him from the departure gate, wearing my father's old jeans and a Joy Division T-shirt in men's XXL. Fifty-seven days ago, I was further according to not only the pencil skirt, bodycon, and halter, but the scale and the measuring tape and those fat-pinching pincers they use at the gym. There is a considerable difference between the girl he saw fifty-seven days ago and this one. Could you even compare the two? You couldn't. You really couldn't. That is a consolation, I think, as I stand in front of the mirror now in my bra and my French cuts and attempt, as I do each evening, to come to grips with certain irrevocable truths. Then I eat several handfuls of flax cereal and fifteen raw, unsalted almonds.

After noting my progress and calculating my daily intake, I decide to phone Tom and see if he's actually booked the plane ticket.

"I did," he says. "Earlier today."

"Oh, great," I say. "That's great."

"You don't sound very excited."

"Of course I am. How could I not be? It's been so long." When he says nothing, I add, "Fifty-seven days." To show him that I've been counting. It matters, this absence.

"You wanted to wait," he says.

I met Tom nearly a year ago on the Dirty List, this online music forum dedicated to fans of Underworld, and we've been in this long-distance thing ever since. I told everyone, including the girl I hate, that Tom and I met at Underworld's last live show in New York before they stopped touring, which is where we actually did meet in person for the first time. Even though I was at my fattest then, he just looked at me, took my hand, and said we should probably line up. Since then, I've seen him every few months. I use most of what I make from my temp jobs after rent to pay for flights, which he splits with me. My mother thinks it's absurd to spend so much money going to see a guy I barely know—or who she thinks I barely know—but since I started losing weight she hasn't said anything. Obviously seeing Tom is good for me. Still, I don't want to see him again until I've broken this, whatever this is. I'm hesitant to call it a plateau.

"Not because I didn't want to see you sooner, though," I tell Tom now. "I just couldn't get away. Because of work." I think of how I Liquid-Papered *bitch* across my stapler in that long stretch before lunch. The paper-clip porn I make in the afternoons. How I killed yesterday looking up Bettie Page screen savers just to torture myself.

"I know," he says. "Well I'm looking forward to it."

I've turned out the light so I can't see the mirror, but it's there, and so is my shape in it, dark and vague in the glass.

"Me too," I say.

Later, after I've hung up and I'm lying awake in bed, I think of the perfect comeback to the salady remark. I put us both back in the bakery and I make her say that I'm salady with clotted cream in each corner of her lips. But instead of replying, Am I? I lean in and in a low voice I say, Listen, you little skank! Not all of us can eat scones and have it turn into more taut littleness! Some of us are forced to eat spring mix in the half-dark of our low-ceilinged studio apartments and still expand inexplicably. Some of us expand at the mere contemplation of what you shovel so carelessly, so dancingly into your smug little mouth. And the way I say it, leaning in like that, with all this edge and darkness in my voice garnered from months of restraint, makes her bow her head in genuine remorse.

On my walk to work the next day, I make a promise to myself. I promise that when the girl I hate asks me out to lunch I'll say No, I'll say No, I'll say No. Then, at around eleven, when she sends me a text that says, Weird Swedish Pizza!! Omnomnom!! I text back, ☺. We go to the Scandinavian café she loves. She orders a sausage-lavender-thyme pizza square the size of her head plus a kanelbulle, a cinnamon bun, for later, for what she calls Secret Eating. I get the fennel-pomegranate-dill salad, which comes undressed in a diamond-shaped bowl. While she's eating the pizza, she watches me forage through limp dill fronds for fennel quarter moons. I try to distract her by making a comment about the weather, how I thought it was supposed to rain today, something to make her look skyward, but her eyes are on me, my fork, the bowl.

"That salad's small," she says.

"Not really," I say, bringing the bowl closer to me. "It only looks small."

But she won't let it be. She lifts her heart-shaped sunglasses, leans forward, peers down into the bowl, and sort of wrinkles her nose like she's just smelled something awful.

"It looks small because it is small," she says, sitting back. She cocks her head to one side, like I'm curious. "How come you got that?"

I say something about how I just like pomegranate seeds, how they're pretty, like rubies.

She stares at me until I feel heat creep up the back of my neck. Then she shrugs. She's wearing this strappy tank that exposes how her shoulders are all bone. She opens her mouth wide and takes a pointedly large bite of pizza, then leans back, chewing, and tilts her tiny face toward the sun.

"I love shun," she says.

That night, while I'm having dinner with Mel at the bistro with the fun salads, I bitch to her about Itsy Bitsy, which is what I call the girl I hate when I'm being funny about how I hate her. I don't even wait until we've gotten our drinks, I just start in while we still have the oversize menus in front of us. I tell Mel about the scones and the Swedish pizza. I tell her about the salady remark. I tell her what I wished I could have told Itsy Bitsy, about scones turning into more taut littleness for some, while others are forced to grow fat on salad. I figure Mel, who's fat now, heavier even than I was at my heaviest, will appreciate how hate-worthy she is. It's what I love most about Mel.

She says, "Itsy Bitsy. I think you've told me about her before. She's the girl who kept eating the lemon slices off your vodka sevens, right?"

"That was Soy Foam. The anorexic from my old work. This is another one, from my new work. And I don't hate her so much anymore."

"Itsy Bitsy?"

"Soy Foam."

Soy Foam was annoying, really annoying, but at least I *got* her. I didn't at first. At first all I saw was this terribly small woman from Accounts who, whenever we'd go to lunch, would order an Americano with steamed soy milk on the side, then eat the foam with a spoon, like soup. Then one night, during happy hour, after devouring all my cocktail garnish, she drunkenly confessed she hadn't had her period in two years and that as a result of premature menopause, she'd had to start shaving her face. After that, I hated her less. But it's different with Itsy Bitsy.

"Sorry. So who's Itsy Bitsy then, Lizzie?"

Beth, I want to correct her. I'm Beth now, not Lizzie. But even though I've told Mel time and time again that I'm not going by Lizzie anymore, she always reverts back to it.

"Itsy Bitsy's the super thin one. With the heart tights. Who makes the Cookie Monster noises."

"Oh," she said. "Right. Well, why do you go to lunch with her if you hate her?"

"We're friends. She's actually really nice aside from this."

I remember how, during my first week, she sort of took me under her wing. Showed me how to use the photocopier. Got me out of a printing jam by banging her fist repeatedly on the lid until it belched out the other half of my report. Once, when I had a tension headache, she pinched my palm between her thumb and forefinger super hard for five minutes because she'd read online that sometimes that helps. Also, she was the only other girl in the office in her midtwenties. The only one who bothered to talk to me, at least. We even have a girl we hate together: Probiotic Yoga Evangelist, this whore from HR. After we caught each other making gag-me faces at her Bikram Changed My Life speech, which she made between spoonfuls of Oikos in the break room, we sort of bonded.

"Yeah," Mel agrees. "I guess that makes it harder."

The waitress comes and I order my heart salad with the poppy seed dressing on the side.

"Heart salad?" Mel asks.

"It's this salad that has heart everything," I say. "Artichoke hearts. Romaine hearts. Hearts of palm. I love it."

Mel orders the roast beef and Havarti scroll with the sweet potato fries. She suggests sharing the baked Camembert appetizer but when I refuse, she doesn't push like she used to. Maybe she's starting to understand that I can't afford to lose what is at best a tenuous, hard-won momentum. I tell her she should get it, though. For herself. It sounds good.

"I can't get it for just me. I'm not *that* much of a pig. I hope."

"I'll have a bite," I offer.

Mel says she shouldn't get it anyway. She should, you know, be good. "Like you." She gives me a half smile.

I tell her I'm honestly not that good. Really, I'm—

"You are," she says. "I wish I had your discipline."

"You did there for a while," I say, looking away.

For a while, Mel was pretty committed, using her mother's old Exercycle, living on Diet Coke and Michelina's Light. In fact, for a while there, Mel began to look like the unstoppable force of nature she was when she was seventeen, the girl who wore black bras you could see through her white Catholic school blouse and who blew all the boys I ever professed to love in her bedroom postered with obscure Goth bands, while I sat in the downstairs den with her mother, who taught me how to cheat at solitaire.

That was a couple of years ago, when we were living together. I was still more or less an agoraphobic whale, switching my major every quarter—from English to French Literature to Art History to Medieval Studies to Film—going to the random lecture when I could bring myself to leave my bedroom, adding and dropping electives like Gaelic, collecting syllabi-like travel brochures for destinations I wasn't sure I wanted to go to. When Mel started losing, I tried to be supportive. I'd say things like, "You look great, but you don't want to go *too* far." You know, things a friend would say to a friend. But Mel would just sip her Diet Coke, sort of smug, like she had a secret, leaving half her salad for the waitress to clear away. She lost steam after a few months though. Couldn't keep it off. Gained it back plus, plus.

"I guess I kind of went too far," Mel says now.

"I did tell you not to go too far," I remind her. "You still look beautiful," I add. I search for something about her to compliment. She is beautiful, of course, but since she gained all that weight back, she's let herself go a little, grooming-wise. Usually she'll wear at least lipstick for me because she knows it depresses me to see her without it, but today her lips are all bare and crackly.

"I love your top," I say at last. It's hideous. One of those tent-like horrors from the plus-size store. There are some iridescent baubles along the neckline, some frothy bits of lace trailing from the cap sleeves, presumably to lessen its resemblance to a shroud.

"I love the sleeve detail."

Mel looks down at the froth, frowning. "It's okay, I guess."

"I think it's nice. It's weird how they seem to have way nicer things at that store than they did back when I had to shop there."

"It's still the same crap," she spits. "They just have more selection is all."

We stab at our ice.

"I love *your* top, though," she says, eyeing my corseted tank. "Siren?"

"Hell's Belles."

"I thought that place closed."

"Nope. Still open. New owner, though."

"Huh. I guess I never really go downtown anymore." Mel moved out of our apartment when she decided to go back to college—she couldn't afford tuition and rent on a music store clerk's salary—and now she lives with her mother back in Misery Saga.

"I used to love shopping there," she says now.

"I remember."

Waiting outside the fitting room while she tried on PVC corsets and velvet empire-waist dresses. The former owner, a corpselike woman named Gruvella, regarding me with eyes the color of skim milk as though I were about to steal something. Not that anything she had would've fit me then, not even the fingerless gloves. Mel finally coming out from behind the white-and-black-striped curtain, twirling for me while I sat in the chair with the clawed armrests, saying, "Great, that looks great."

"I still remember that black bell-sleeved dress you got there. The one you wore to the prom with the spider tights."

"The Bella. I forgot about that dress. God, good memory."

The waitress brings our food. She's forgotten to put my poppy seed dressing on the side, which often happens with this waitress and sometimes? Honestly? I think maybe she does it on purpose just to fuck with me. I tell her about it and she says, "Oh, well, she *could* change it for me," and I say, "Could you?" And I tell Mel to go ahead and start without me.

"She sounds pretty annoying," Mel says. "Sadistic, even."

"Itsy Bitsy? She is." I tell Mel that I'm starting to think she befriended me to make herself feel good. To feel extra bitsy. That I think she actually gets off on it, eating copiously in front of me while

I eat nothing, and pointing out how I'm eating nothing while she's eating copiously.

"I guess that's possible," Mel says. She picks up her fork and knife, then lowers them. "I feel bad about starting without you. You sure you don't want at least some fries while you wait?"

I tell her I better not. I've been on such a slippery slope lately.

Mel bites into her scroll. "You look the shame to me," she says. "Shkinnier, even."

"I wish. I'm pretty sure I've plateaued. And I'm flying out to see Tom soon."

"I don't know if I support you doing this for Tom."

"I'm not. It's just useful to have a date in mind. To work toward. You know?"

Mel keeps eating her scroll.

"This is for me," I add.

"Good. Because he should love you the way you are."

"He does."

"Good." Mel nods, and takes a bite of scroll. "I'm glad that one of these Internet things finally worked out for you. I was worried he'd be another creep. Like that soap opera guy in the wheelchair. God, what was his name? Something awful. Blair or something."

"Blake."

"Or that one from before from Colorado who kept claiming he'd dated international models. What a liar. And a loser."

"Yeah," I say, cutting into an artichoke heart. "How are things with Henry?"

She makes a face. "The same. I don't really want to talk about it, if that's okay."

"Of course. Well. Anyone you hate these days?"

Mel cuts a large piece of scroll. Then she says there are people who annoy her. Who seriously, seriously annoy her. But no, no one worthy of hate. Hating requires a lot of energy; she's so tired these days.

"I know what you mean," I say. "I'm tired too."

Speaking of which, Mel says, she has an early class tomorrow.

I ask her if she'd like me to drive her home after dinner, but she says it's fine. Really.

I tell her I'm happy to at least drive her to the bus station closer to her house, that I'd really hate for her to have to take two buses at night. It's such a long ride to Misery Saga, and besides, I feel like I never see her anymore. Like she's disappeared.

"I haven't *disappeared*," she says. "But I know what you mean. I feel like I never see you anymore either."

On the ride to the bus station, to make her laugh, I tell Mel about Aggressively Naked, this woman who works out at my gym who does all of her post-workout grooming naked. She brushes her hair naked. She uses her straightening iron naked. Eyelash curler and mascara naked. Rings, necklace, and even bracelets naked. Only after she's got herself totally primped will she put on her clothes.

"Isn't that annoying?"

"It is," Mel agrees.

"I can't believe I forgot to tell you earlier. Also, she's got this body you wouldn't believe. Like, I knew just by her body she didn't speak English. I knew that when she opened her mouth, something like Danish would come out."

"Oh my god, stop," she says, mock-covering her ears. "Just stop."

Once we get to the bus station, I insist on holding Mel in the car until the bus comes. She takes her bus pass out of her little change purse to be at the ready. I tell her I love her change purse, even though there is really nothing distinctive about it. It's just a change purse. Black leather with a little zip.

I ask her if she's sure she doesn't want me to take her home, the bus sucks. She says she actually doesn't mind it, that ever since she moved back in with her mother, she uses the bus for Me Time. Me Time for Mel has always been a dark fantasy novel and some ethereal dark wave on her iPod. It comforts me that this has never changed.

I know she wouldn't care for most of the things I listen to now but I have a mix I keep in the car of songs we used to listen to together, and I put this on for the ride. The track playing now is "Annwyn, Beneath the Waves" by Faith and the Muse. I haven't listened to them in a while but now I turn it up.

"I love this song," I say, turning to look at her.

She says nothing.

"Remember the first time we saw these guys?"

She smiles now at the windshield. "Yeah."

"How we lined up at the door at like three in the afternoon because we figured everyone would want to see them, that there'd be this huge line, but it was just us? For like hours on the sidewalk waiting? No one else showed up until like seven."

"We got there early to get a table. We always did that for shows."

I thought of how we'd just sit there all afternoon, melting in the sun, listening to the album we were about to hear live on continuous loop on our respective Discmans. Me sweating profusely in the most

Gothic ensemble I could patch together at my size, which was usually fishnet tights worn as a top under one of my mother's black night slips, Mel fully decked out in one of her Siren ensembles, lipstick black, eye makeup red and three times more elaborate than mine.

"We were cute," she says now, meaning it.

I want to talk to her more, but she's spotted the bus in the distance, so I say okay, good-bye, and tell her I'll text her later, but she's already out of the car, running toward the stop.

Tonight, as I do my assessment in front of the mirror, it seems there are more truths to come to grips with. Sometimes this happens. How many there are often depends on lighting. Not on how much, but on how it's hitting me, on how it's hitting certain parts. Three weeks and three days left until I fly there. He says he loves me right now. He claims he already loved me the moment he first saw me at Underworld. When I first saw him I remember thinking I must have been at least three times his size; he was so thin and pale, he looked like he was barely there, like a ghost, like I'd dreamed him. I remember thinking he was beautiful, but I didn't look at him very much. In fact, I looked at him so little that first time that when I was away from him, I couldn't exactly recall his face. In my memory, his features were slippery, vague. His eyes kept changing color, like in the song by New Order. But he claims that he loved me then and that he fell in love with me before that night even, before he even saw me, that he loved me from that night 103 days ago when we switched from online chats about music to phone conversations about music and I would sit here in my studio apartment, my phone crooked in my sweating neck, enumerating the many reasons why I loved this or that band or book or film and then he would enumerate his. From even before that when all I was was a small, snarky post he saw on the Dirty List at three a.m. to which he felt compelled to respond. That was nearly a year ago, and nearly a year ago, I was much further from my goal indeed. Probably I was Mel's size then. Now I'm almost half that.

After noting my progress, I lie in bed in my studio, thinking of Mel while I eat a bar of 72 percent dark chocolate square by square. I picture her in her mother's Misery Saga house filled with all those strange breeds of orchid. I picture her walking up the creaking steps toward her blood-colored childhood bedroom, surrounded by walls of obscure fantasy novels and towers of even more obscure dark wave CDs whose precise configuration I used to know by heart. With a hand on my stomach, I imagine her lying on her back in the too-small bed, a bed we slept on together so many nights in my teens, the twin mattress sagging beneath her, a moon through the window silhouetting her, the gentle rise and fall of her immense stomach, her slight snore, until my eyes close.

In the morning, when I step on the scale, I steel myself for the sight of the needle going up (that chocolate), but to my astonishment, it's tipped down.

At the office, it's the usual midmorning drudgery. I'm doing the seven steps it takes to open the mail while drinking black coffee. Itsy Bitsy is scheduling, while secret-eating a kardemummabullar, a cardamom bun, at her desk. She's pretending to secret-eat for my sake, to make me laugh, like look what a pig she is, she can't even wait until lunch. She over-crackles the paper bag, does shifty eyes before each superbite. She's wearing this sixties minidress with matching white go-go boots like something stitched out of my nightmares. Seeing me watch her, she waves, her cheeks plump with kardemummabullar. I wave back, and the hate I feel is bottomless. The hate could drown us both. She swallows and mouths, Lunch, at me like it's a question and I nod in spite of myself.

In that photo of my father and me, the one where I'm as small as the girl I hate, the one where he is gazing down at me with such love and incomprehension, the one taken before he left and before I grew up heavy like my mother, I'm looking right into the camera. It might have been the last time I looked right into a lens and smiled with no reservations, with no shame. He showed me this photo recently, when we met for a strained lunch on my last birthday, when I was at my biggest, before I met Tom, before I started losing. He included it in an album of photos that he gave me as part of my birthday gift, one that was presumably meant to show me that I hadn't always been fat. Look. See? Where did I get this idea? Maybe from my mother, he said. Probably it was all from my mother. *She* always struggled. But you? Look. But all I could see was the caption sticker above the photo that read, "Great Time Every Time," which I could never picture my father purchasing, let alone pasting decoratively into an album. Which is how I knew he hadn't put the album together himself. Probably he'd had one of his secretary-mistresses do it, or maybe it was a temp like me and the girl I hate.

My phone buzzes. She's just texted me: "Pineapple orgy at Kilimanjaro! Om-nom-nom-nom!!!! }8D."

I've eaten there with her before. It's this sandwich and cake shop that has nothing to do with Africa, despite its name and decor. Under a black-and-white still of Serengeti cranes, I'll watch her eat a monster-size ham and Gruyère panini with pineapple chutney, slurp down a mango, strawberry, and pineapple smoothie, then scarf a slice of pineapple upside-down cake. By the time the waitress sets that slice in front of her, I'll have finished eating half of my veggie delite wrap, even though I will eat as slowly as possible. By the time she cuts into her cake, my hands will be empty. And with her mouth full of cake, she'll say something about how I've only eaten half the wrap. She might even point. She might even reach across the table and point at it, my sad, uneaten other half. And I'll have to say something awkward about wanting to save this other half for later, which we'll both know is a lie. I might even ask the waitress for a to-go bag, but she won't be fooled. She'll look at me like, Huh, and take another bite of pineapple cake. I text back, ;D, and as I do this, the hate shifts, spreads its wings in me, becomes almost electric, like love.

I Want Too Much

One of these days I'm probably going to kill Trixie. I have my reasons. I can hear her squawking to another customer just beyond the fitting room door, which isn't actually a door it's a curtain, it's a dark red curtain like a Lynchian portal to hell. On the other side, Trixie is telling some woman how, with some cute boots, that skirt could really be cute. Or a cute shirt! What about a cute shirt? What about a cute shirt *and* cute boots?! So cute.

Something happens inside me whenever Trixie says the word *cute*. My shoulders meet my ears. Heat crackles up my arms. And I grow afraid behind my curtain, bracing myself for the moment when the shrill edge of her voice becomes pointed in my direction. Because it's only a matter of time. The robin's egg spaghetti strap number she chose for me has my tits in a stranglehold and she'll be coming to check on that soon. There's a soft quick click of heels, the papery rustle of overly moussed hair, a long-nailed hand tugging on the curtain.

Then: "How are we doing in here?"

"Fine," I say.

Anyone else would be daunted, even offended by my tone. It's awful and I never use it on anyone but Trixie. But she bounces back just fine.

"Okay," she says. Then: "Can I see?"

Her voice rises to an impossible shrillness on the *see*. I can feel her *see* in my teeth roots.

"*No*," I say.

Because Trixie never helps. Because of Trixie, I have already made several regrettable purchases.

"No?" she repeats.

She knows my no isn't a real no. She knows it's the no of a petulant child refusing to play her part. It's true that when it comes to shopping for clothes, I have a history of having a bad attitude. That's what my mother said to me all the time. *You have a bad attitude. You're making this harder than it has to be.* Especially now that I've started losing, she seems to think everything looks good on me and is particularly intolerant of my complaints.

Trixie's cooing at me to come out, come out, so I do, I pull back the curtain and stand before the mirror under the track lighting, Trixie hovering behind me.

She looks me up and down, her head cocked to one side.

"Cute," she says. But this means nothing. To Trixie, even the apocalypse is cute. Scorched earth. Galloping black horses foaming at the mouth. The shadow of the scythe-wielding dealer of Fate bearing down on her. All super cute.

But the dress isn't. There are huge gaps between the front metal teeth, where my chest is pulling the fabric in opposite directions. When I point this out, Trixie sort of wrinkles her nose, looks troubled, squinty. I've cast clouds over her clear horizon. It's not the first time.

"Can't you see this gap here?" I ask Trixie, pointing to my chest.

"Not really," Trixie says. Why is Trixie so eager to see when she can't see at all?

"*Here?* Right *here?*" I say, thumping at my own dress-throttled chest. You're telling me you don't *see* that?

She squints hard at my chest, sort of shakes her head, like she's confused. Then her eyes suddenly brighten.

"You know what *I* would do?"

And that's the thing with Trixie. She always has a solution.

"You could just put a cute necklace! With a pendant that covers this part? Or a scarf! What about a scarf and tie it here?" she says, her fingers hovering over the wide space between the teeth. She asks me if she can show me a scarf?

What I want to say to Trixie is, Trixie? Why do I come here? Why do I subject myself to this humiliation? I don't deserve this, Trixie. I ate turkey in hydroponic lettuce wraps for a whole year. I Gazelled. Do you know what a Gazelle is, Trixie? It's a cardiovascular machine that's a hybrid of a treadmill and an elliptical. But then I look at her blinking optimistically at me from behind what have to be false eyelashes and I know she'll have no idea what I'm talking about.

So I say, "Show me the scarf."

She trots off happily to get the scarf.

Beside me is another woman also being serviced by Trixie. The woman has a big ass and she's wearing jeans that are far too tight for it. It was Trixie who chose these jeans, clearly. Now Trixie has coaxed this woman out from behind her curtain and dragged her under the track lighting, which sheds a light that only Trixie looks good in. And on her way to pick up my scarf, she looks at this woman muffin-topping out of her jeans and says, Cute!! And when the woman says, What about my ass? Trixie says, What about a belt?

Like a big belt! And some cute boots. With a big belt and some cute boots, she'd be saved from her own ass. She'll go grab some belts.

But this woman isn't like me. She's grateful. She believes in Trixie's solutions. She waits patiently for the belts, turning herself this way and that, and I know she's telling herself that her ass doesn't look that big, not that big after all.

But it does is the thing.

Trixie is now fastening the scarf around my neck like a flaccid noose and I feel my chest getting red and patchy and hot underneath her hands. She is uncomfortably close. I can smell all of her smells: hair products and Greek cooking and enthusiasm.

The pattern of the scarf doesn't at all match the pattern of the dress. I'm about to say something about that but Trixie anticipates this and cuts me off.

"This is just to *show* you," she explains, looping it around my neck. "This is just so you'll *see*."

As she ties it around my neck, she accidentally scrapes me with a nail.

"Oops. Sorry."

The scarf covers the gap in the front teeth of the dress but otherwise looks ridiculous. As I knew it would.

But Trixie looks terribly pleased with herself. Like she's a genius or something. Like by tying this mismatching scarf around my neck, a scarf that looks ridiculous with the dress not just in pattern but in principle, she's shown me a solution to the problem of my flesh.

"See?"

"Yeah," I say, tugging on the scarf like it's choking me. "The thing is? I don't want to have to wear a scarf to wear this dress. Or a necklace. Or anything else. I just want—"

Trixie raises a threaded eyebrow, waiting.

"I just want to, you know, *wear* it. . . ."

"Oh," she says, furrowing her brow. She gives me a look like perhaps given my size and all, I want too much?

I wrench off her knotted handiwork, revealing the gap in the teeth again. The other woman, the big-assed one in the too-tight jeans who is being placated with belts, looks at me like I'm being mutinous.

"Because it really is too tight, isn't it? I mean, really?"

My eyes say, Say it, Trixie. Say it for both of us.

She smiles, looks both ways like a caged animal before she bores her eyes into me and nods a little. It's a barely perceptible tilt of the head, as if being this honest isn't allowed but she'll make an exception just this once.

Then she adds, aloud: "I don't think so. Not if you wore a scarf. But you don't want to wear a scarf, you said, so . . ."

She shrugs. Like that's the last trick in her bag of tricks.

She turns on her heel and trots off to get more belts for the big-assed woman.

And I feel suddenly deserted. Discarded. Cast off like an ill-fitting dress. Suddenly I want to bathe in the light of Trixie's eyes again. I want her to ask me to turn for her. I want her to fix her eyes, the eyes where everything fits, where it's just a matter of the right accessory, the right attitude, on me. I want my mother's eyes.

As Trixie walks off, she puts a hand on the big-assed woman's shoulder and squeezes and says she won't be a minute with those belts. And the woman glows, basking in Trixie's attention. She says, "No problem at all," her eyes moony with love as she turns to once more admire her terrible ass in the mirror.

My Mother's Idea of Sexy

Tonight, she's trussed me up in a one-strap midriff-baring bit of turquoise gauze she bought me just this afternoon at The Rack. Paired it with skintight low-risers and pink strappy heels from Payless that are like a shoe version of a Frederick's of Hollywood thong.

"I don't know about this outfit," I tell my mother, frowning at the tentacles sprouting from my left shoulder. We're at this seafood place on the wharf because she thinks fish is my secret. A touristy place in the city she recently moved to on the west coast. A table by the window so she can watch for her friends. My wide slash of bared stomach feels like an emergency no one is attending to, my feet like they're doing bad porn under the table. Shoulder and hip still buzzing from where she cut the price tag loops off with a butter knife. Mother, these clothes are ridiculous, I should have said. They mock us both. I can dress myself. I'm a twenty-six-year-old woman. Instead, I say, "You think maybe it's too much?"

My mother sits across from me under a giant net full of plastic crustaceans, watching me ignore the fact of the bread basket and the crab dip appetizer, my fingers braided over my empty side plate. She eyes me from gauzy tentacles to bare stomach. She says, "What do you mean 'too much'? How is it *too much*? Trust me."

She riffles through the bread basket absently. "Those shoes." She shakes her head. "Shit. Show me again?"

I bring one foot out from under the table and wiggle it at her.

"They're going to flip when they see you, Elizabeth, flllip."

"They hurt."

"Humor me."

I watch her pile her slab of sourdough thickly with crab dip. Her patchy red face. Her preternaturally bright eyes. It's in my throat to ask her if she's checked her blood sugar today. Instead, I look out the window at the mongers throwing fish for show, the Vietnamese women rearranging flowers with delicate hands. I pour a mound of salt onto the table and begin raking it with my fork tines, my latest non-eating way of eating. "So who am I meeting tonight again?"

"Just some people from the office," she says, dusting crumbs off the front of her dress. She moved out here to take a corporate job, much higher paying than the middle-management hospitality positions she's held most of my life. "Dawn, Pam, Denise. Maybe one or two others."

"Okay," I say, giving up on the salt and screwing a cigarette into my mouth, fishing through my purse for a lighter. My mother brings a candle to my unlit tip.

"Don't sit like that, though," she says.

"Like what?"

"Slouched like that." She does an impression of me, hunching her hulking shoulders forward, causing her costume jewelry to jangle. She's wearing the red set today: rings, necklace, bracelets. All but the oversize clip-ons, which she just affixed to my lobes in the restroom because It still needs something.

I look at her from her spiked hair to the hillocks of her arms swathed in Lane Bryant lace. Mutinous words rise in my throat. I swallow them. Straighten.

"This is my daughter," she announces when they arrive, gesturing toward me like I am a just-turned letter in *Wheel of Fortune* and she is Vanna White. "She's just visiting. Stopping by on her way to her boyfriend's—sorry, fiancé! You guys remember."

"Quite the ensemble," one of her friends offers. Five of them, not three. Their smiles thin as Communion wafers. Looking at me in a way that makes me want to snatch my mother's shawl and drape it over my bared shoulders. Or at least wrap my arms around my exposed midriff, but she would never forgive me. Instead, I smile.

"Isn't it?" my mother says, pleased as punch, and I hear the words before they even bloom on her lips: "Show them."

"Up, though. Stand up." Using her hands like she's a preacher raising the dead, her bracelets of blown glass clacking against her wrists. "Turn so they can see the back?"

I turn with my hands out to my sides, staggering slightly. The turquoise shoulder tentacles swell and float around me. I turn until I hear the word *beautiful* erupt from her friend Dawn like a belch.

"Isn't she?" says my mother.

Isn't she is my cue. I fall back into my chair, the tentacles billowing then settling, the women and I exchanging embarrassed smiles. I take a long sip of Diet Coke, my mother in my eye corner, her face twisted by pride, her features all tied in little bows of glee.

"Show them your bicep," she says.

"Mom. No." Like I'm above such a request, but actually the first thing I did when I got off the plane was show my mother my biceps.

Look!

I see, I see!

"Works out all the time now," my mother continues. "Had to get a trial membership at the gym across the street just so she'd agree to visit me."

"*Mom*. That isn't tr—"

"Walks too. Two, three times a day. All along the lake," she says, marching her index and middle finger across the air like they're my legs. "Fast. I've gone with her a couple of times but I can't keep up."

"You can keep up," I say, even as I recall marching forward, trying to be oblivious to my mother breathless behind me, my eyes fixed straight ahead, until I felt guilty and turned back. She was standing several yards away, her broad back heaving. Pretending to examine shells on the beach.

"It's those legs," she says, looking down at my new spiked heels. "Those legs, I can't compete."

I pretend to look out the window but it's too dark now to see anything but my own slumped, shoulder-tentacled silhouette, my mother's wild gesticulations, the indulgent nods of her acquaintances. I excuse myself to go to the restroom, aware of all their eyes on me as I teeter away from the table.

"You were great, just great," my mother says as we stroll through the market, arm in arm, later. She walks me along the stalls like she's leading me down the aisle, loving how I'm immune to the plenty. How I wrinkle my nose, shake my head at everything but a Fuji and some fish for later, while she helps herself to fistfuls of whatever samples are there for the taking. We go to the monger's, where I buy my four ounces of whatever's fresh. She waits, watching me, and I feel the blaze of her eyes on my profile.

"When you went to the bathroom? They couldn't stop talking about how beautiful you were. Couldn't stop."

"That's nice."

"Not just *nice*," my mother says, steering me toward the flower stalls, where she treats me to a bouquet of stargazers. For my daughter, she tells the woman behind the tin pails brimming with blossoms. I smile. Me, I'm the daughter, yes. We watch her gather the stems while my mother rubs my exposed husk of shoulder like it's a genie lamp.

"So tomorrow night? You'll meet me at my work. Then we'll go to the mussel place."

She's turned toward me to see how I'm taking this, but I keep staring straight ahead at the windshield. We're in the car going home and the highway wind is whipping my hair into my eyes, making them tear. I'm trying to light a cigarette but keep lighting my split ends instead. "Careful," my mother says. She rented a red Sebring convertible especially for my visit. "I want the wind in my hair," she explained, tugging her black pomaded spikes, immovable even in a gale.

"Why can't I just meet you at the mussel place?" I ask her now.

She closes her eyes, sighs like I've just made her very tired. "Just meet me at my work first. Okay? Indulge me. Can you just do that?"

A bandage dress the color of Pepto-Bismol. She must have laid it out for me on her bed before she left for work in the morning. I stare at it from the doorframe in the French cuts she bought me the other day at Target, a cigarette turning to ash between my lips, my morning Fuji in my fist. All afternoon, I dare Mick Jagger, her obese Abyssinian, to walk all over the dress, but he doesn't, even when I pick him up and place him on top of it. She took photos of me in it the other day with her cheap yellow disposable. Some with me leaning against her stove surrounded on all sides by her chef-themed kitchen accessories. Some on her balcony surrounded by her pots of dying purple flowers, the lake blazing behind me. In all of them, I look like the smug but uncertain solution to a stomach problem. I see she's placed a pair of discounted strappy slingbacks the color of iridescent vomit on the floor close by.

"Jesus," my mother says, shaking her head as, later that afternoon, I lurch toward her in the vomit heels. In her cubicle, she takes a lighter to the plastic price tag loop because I forgot to take care of this detail at home (I always forget these details *why*, exactly? her eyes ask me). Makes me switch lips at the last minute from Rebel to Craving. "Better," she says, "But blot. Little more? *Yes.*"

In my effort to show them the back, my hip bumps against the table, making the mussels clack in their bowls. Unlike the group yesterday, these are mostly men. I nearly lose my balance turning, but one of them catches me with a firm grip.

"Whoa," he says with a laugh. "Careful there. Elizabeth, isn't it? Your mother's told us so much about you."

I flop back down in my chair, screwing a cigarette between my lips, smile boozily at her semicircle of bosses. "Has she?" He pours me another glass of white, his eyes doing a downward graze along the bandages, while my mother pats my knee under the table.

"She's gotten into dancing now," she's telling her bosses. She has so many bosses these days, she told me earlier, I wouldn't believe it. Can't keep them straight, she confided in the bathroom as she marched me into and then out of a cloud of Angel. "Belly dancing, of all things. Belly, isn't it, Elizabeth?"

My mother looks at me, her eyes a shin kick.

"Belly," I affirm, the cigarette dangling unlit from my lips. One of her bosses pours me another drink, even though I'm reeling from the first two.

"How exotic," the one female in the group offers, slightly sourly. "Maybe you could teach us some moves sometime."

"Maybe."

"Oh! Show them!" my mother says. "She showed me last night." She does an awkward impression of snake arms, causing the sleeves of her lace coverall to rise up her forearms. She smooths them down, then goes back to prying open mussels. "Didn't you?"

"Yeah."

I don't know what possessed me to undulate in front of my mother last night while she sat on her flower-patterned couch and watched, her palm pressed firmly on the armrest, Mick Jagger meowing in her large lap.

"I'd love to see," a boss says.

"Room right here," another one says, waving a hand at the space beside him.

"Little shy," my mother says, rubbing my back vigorously, then patting it gently.

The boss who'd love to see gives me a smile like a flickering light. "Shouldn't be."

After a while, they forget I'm here, thank heaven. Hairy hands braided over mountains of glossy disemboweled black shells. Lost in drunken shoptalk. Stopped refilling my glass. I look out the window for the water but all I see is my own swaying reflection. *Who are you and what have you done with my daughter?* she said to me in the market earlier, as I ordered my four ounces from the monger. The package is still in my purse, along with an apple for later. *Seriously who are you?*

In the window's reflection, I see my mother is no longer part of the shoptalk. She's nodding and murmuring *Yeah* every now and then, but out of the corner of her eye, she's watching me light a match with one hand.

"I'll have one of those," she says to me now from across the table, eyeing my cigarette pack.

I look up at her. Her freshly shorn black spiked hair like Liz Taylor meets sea urchin. Each spike slicked crisp with pomade. Snow White skin I was always jealous of. Mouth the color of black plum flesh and full like a fish's. Eyes brimming with odd gold flecks, the left one slightly lazy. The weird slope of her slender nose, broken by a baseball when she was young because she used to play catcher without a mask. My mother's face has always been something she just shrugs off. Whenever anyone calls her beautiful, she shakes her head, bats her hand, her fish lips curling to one side. Like, Whatever. Fuck you. On to something else, please.

I shake the pack at her now in offering, though I know she shouldn't. Her heart, the water in her lungs, and I know she's not telling me the half of it. How she gripped the balcony railing last night. Breathing like she was drowning.

Are you okay? I called from the couch.

Fine, fine.

You sure?

Trust me.

"You can afford to lose one?" she asks me now, withdrawing a cigarette.

I can't, really. I've only got a couple left. And what's even more annoying is how she doesn't inhale, just puffs. But I say, "Sure."

I light it for her with my one-handed trick. She flinches slightly at this.

"Thanks," she says, puffing on it like it's a cigar. She returns to nodding at her head buyer, Rich, who is asking if she and I have ever been sailing.

"Never," my mother lies, still watching me out of the corner of her eye.

"Never?!" Rich says. Oh well, we need to fix that. Only way to see the city. And he has a boat. If we're interested?

We are.

On the way home, she takes an off-ramp, gets herself a large Frosty from a Wendy's drive-through. "You want anything?"

"Diet Coke, lots of ice, make sure lots of ice."

"MAKE SURE LOTS OF ICE!" she roars into the drive-through window. Then, turning to me, "Rich loved you, you know.

And he's a tough customer, trust me. My boss for a year and I still don't know what he thinks of me."

"Probably just being polite," I say.

"You don't just say the things they said to say them. You say a lot of things but not the things they said. Not the way they said them," she insists.

She parks in the Wendy's lot, eats the Frosty guiltily beside me while I sway in the passenger seat, swimmy from the wine, gripping the Diet Coke like it's a buoy. I don't mention diabetes. I don't ask about blood sugar. Instead, I let her eat, the mouth of the giant cup close to her lips.

She sighs into her cup, waggles it at me. "This is okay, right? Just milk and ice?"

"Right," I say. I stare at the road ahead.

When she pulls out of the parking lot, I notice she's driving very slowly, squinting hard at the road.

"How come you're driving so slow?"

She's quiet for a while, then, "I can't feel my feet," she says to the windshield. "Right now."

"That's still happening?" I turn to look at her but her profile gives nothing away. "Mom? That's still happening? Are you going to a doctor for it?"

She's shaking her head at the windshield. "I'll be fine. Still be able to go dancing tomorrow night."

"Dancing? I think we should take it easy."

"It's your last night here before Tom comes. We can have a quiet day on Friday. Just you and me. How does that sound?"

A banana yellow minidress she hasn't worn since the Stones came out with "Satisfaction." Thigh-high white boots. *Fifteen, sixteen I was then, damn I looked good you have no idea.* Matching headband sits on the counter, but I won't put that on unless she forces me. "Paint It Black" skipping on the small stereo on her night table because *We need music for this.* You're a grown woman, you have a choice in this, I remind myself in the mirror. *Show me!* she's calling from the other side of the bathroom door. I'm staring at her crown dentures in the zombie glass full of food-flecked water she keeps by the sink, my hands gripping the bathroom counter. The used pumice stone in the soap dish, which she rubs hard against her heels each night. I hear the sound through the wall but try to convince myself it's something else. How long has it been since you can't feel your feet? is a question I can't bring myself to ask her. Dusty baskets of untouched bath salts, gels, and crystals that smell like too-sweet sick positioned around the unwashed sink for show. The air in here is thick with masked illness and the Fendi she sprays too heavily on her neck in the morning. The smell of it smothers me now, but after she dies, if I catch what I think is even a whiff of it in the street, I'll follow it.

Show me!

I stare at the soiled nightgowns hanging from a silver hook on the back of her bathroom door. Feel the fact of her on the other side, lying belly down on her brass bed, chin on her fists, waiting. The same bed she lay across when I first started losing, watching me turn in her vintage Yves Saint Laurent, then her vintage Dior, neither of which she'd worn since she'd had her jaw wired after giving birth to me. She did it to shed her baby weight. For a few weeks she was a sickly, smiling husk of herself, then back up forever. But she keeps them in the back of her closet still, these monochromatic suits heavy as chain mail, each smelling of a variation of the same sweat, a different discontinued perfume. Turn, she said then, watching me model them when I was fourteen. Chin on her fists then too, shaking her head then too, as I turned and turned for her, seeing the prints of Marilyn and Audrey she had bought and framed and nailed to my bedroom walls. It was years before I'd replace them all with a map of Ireland and a poster of Tori Amos holding a shotgun on a patio full of snakes.

"Show me?" My mother's still calling and calling from the bed.

After, she sits with me on the balcony, as I eat my four ounces of scrod and sip at the pre-dancing cocktail she made especially for me, a French 75 she shook and strained into an ornate crystal flute from the back of her glass hutch. It's topped with a lemon peel she knifed into an elegant twist. "Am I a good bartender or what?"

"You're not having one?" I ask her.

"I'm good," she says, waggling her club soda at me, which she also poured into a champagne flute to make it festive. She's watching me eat and sip, among the vases of stargazers we keep forgetting to water, like I'm on-the-edge-of-your-seat television.

"What?" I ask her, keeping my eyes on the dusk. The sky is the color of a busted peach over the shimmer of lake.

"Nothing. How is it?"

I shrug. "Good."

"Good." She's not eating or drinking, just watching. Arms folded. Refolded. Opening and closing her mouth with me. Take your time. *Enjoy* it. "So. Tom, huh?"

"Yup."

"When will he be here, again?"

"Friday night."

"Friday night. Tomorrow," she says. "Has your father met him yet?"

"No."

She looks pleased about this.

"How is your father?"

"Fine."

"He must be proud of you."

My father has always felt that being fat was a choice. When I was in college I would sometimes meet him for lunch or coffee, and he would stare at my extra flesh like it was some weird piece of clothing I was wearing just to annoy him. Like my fat was an elaborate turban or Mel's zombie tiara or some anarchy flag that, in my impetuous youth, I was choosing to hold up and wave in his face. Not really part of me, just something I was doing to rebel, prove him wrong. I started seeing him even less. Now, I wouldn't say he's proud of me. As far as he is concerned, things have just become as they should be. I've finally put down the flag. Taken off the turban. Case closed. Good for me.

"I guess he is."

"He never really notices. But he notices. We should do lunch. Or brunch. Someplace by the water. Depending on what your beau would like. What are you going to wear?"

The last time Tom picked me up from the airport, I was wearing a black twinset and a red fishtail skirt I drown in now. Three-hole Docs with thick rubber soles that deeply depress my mother. *Don't they depress you?* A satchel with a skull Liquid-Papered on the front flap slapping against my broad thigh.

"Not sure yet."

"You're really going to move out there, huh?"

"Eventually. We can't do the long-distance thing forever. And because of his job he can't move to where I am."

"What about your job?"

"I can temp anywhere. Or there are bookstores. Cafés."

"Cafés? But didn't you get a degree in . . . what was it? Medieval something, right?"

French literature, though it was art history in the end. And I didn't finish, exactly.

"Something like that. Don't worry, I can get another job."

"Still. All the way out there."

I look at the lake, thinking of the broad expanse of red desert where he lives in the Southwest, of strange yellow sky, a body of salt water upon which even a plane could float. The way he looks at me, his gaze serene and unflinching.

"I like it out there," I tell my mother.

"But how are you going to survive in the desert when all you eat is fish?" She looks at my scrod. "What kind's that one?"

Just four ounces, I told the monger from across the icy trays of splayed fish, tentacles, and live crustaceans. As he was wrapping it up in brown paper, he threw in a butterflied fillet of another slim fish I didn't recognize, its head still on. I looked at its milky eye, its open mouth full of tiny little teeth like claws, then at him grinning.

Trust me, he said.

"Well," my mother says to me, "should we get ready?"

In the bedroom, later that night, she flips channels until we find an old Hepburn I haven't seen. "You haven't *seen* this?"

Though she claims it's her favorite, she isn't watching the screen. She's watching my face to see if I'm catching all the lovely bits, all the lines she's memorized. I keep my features immobile as I sit by the sliding glass balcony door, her crystal ashtray between my splayed legs, blowing smoke rings into the crack between the door and the frame. I pretend I don't feel her watching me. "This is so nice," says my mother, breathless on the bed. "I like this. Taking it easy."

You sure you're okay just sitting here? I asked her tonight at the salsa club, sweat dripping from my chin into her cranberry and soda with lime.

I'm having a ball, she said, twiddling her toes and taking a sip of her drink as if to show me what a ball it was. You go back out there, she said. Go back, go back! All night, she watched from a table while on the dance floor, I got passed from one partner to the next. Turns they didn't cover in the free salsa lesson tripped me up, but I did my best to follow, just follow, it's easy, or so all the panther-footed men told me. Don't *try* so hard, said a man in a black guayabera patterned with red flames when I lost my footing on a spin. You're trying too hard, he said. To be all sexy. With your hips. Just listen to the music. Just follow the beat. Annoyed with him, I went back to my mother.

Can we go home now, please?

But she wouldn't leave until the floor had emptied of men and the band had begun to pack up. I thought for sure she would want to go home after that, but when I mentioned it, she said, Are you kidding? The night's young! Go where you would go if I wasn't here, if you were with friends. The truth is I'd go home. Instead, she retrieved a city weekly from a trash can on the corner, made me hunt for a Goth night in Capitol Hill.

You sure about this? I asked her as she handed two fivers to a man in bondage gear who stamped black snakes on our hands.

Go on, my mother said over the blare of German industrial, giving me a small push into the swishing columns of dust-ridden light. She watched me turn under the mirror ball through the smoke from a table just off the dance floor, chin on her fists. I spun though my limbs ached, counting the songs off in my head, until I felt I'd made it if not worth her while, then at least worth the price of two covers.

She scoops up her meowing cat and puts him on the bed beside her. "Where's his collar?"

I tore the hideous rhinestone monstrosity from his neck and threw it over the balcony railing while she was at work the other day. Watched it disappear between the tall pines, then fall with a plop into the dark water. The bell made a pleasant tinkling sound all the way down.

"Don't know," I say now. "Must have taken it off."

"He can't do that. Not by himself. Not the way I put it on."

"Well maybe it came loose or something. How are your feet?" I ask her, looking at them still encased in the Keds.

Her eyes flit from my neck to the television, where Audrey's ice-cream cone has just fallen into the Seine.

"Fine," she says, not looking back at me.

I don't know how long I've been standing here dangerously close to the ice beds full of bleeding fish and live crustaceans, watching them gut and clean slabs of salmon and pike, daring them to spill something on me. Afternoon. I'm alone. Above me, the gray sky is spinning but I ignore that and the fact of the terribly soft asphalt under my feet.

Just need to use the restroom, I told my mother and Tom, who are waiting for me now at a table by the window, by the water.

So you have a view, she told him. You need to have a view.

Be back in a minute, I told them.

Now I rock back on my heels, not the heels she laid out for me this morning. Not the dress she laid out for me either. This one's a white and black Max Azria that looks like the dress Grace Kelly wears in *Rear Window*. When I came out of the fitting room in it, my mother said nothing for a full minute, then she said, You're going to get raped. I have to keep my back straight if I want to keep the sweetheart neckline from sliding down, which it did twice in the fitting room. Tricky, my mother said, standing in the slit between the curtains. But if you can pull it off? Shit. I wanted to wear a cardigan with it, but my mother said, That'll ruin it—just keep your back straight and your arms close to your sides like this. Like this. Exactly. Five-inch red patent leather Guess heels. Just remember to take the price stickers off, she said. I didn't. They're still on the soles, black Sharpie slashes over the original price, the half-off price in red ink.

I teeter closer to the stall, evaluating the different men behind the glass case, their biceps flexing as they throw and sing, throw and sing.

I pick the one with the Hellraiser hair and the missing incisor and the eyes the no-color of oceans. We'll do it in the dark of the truck full of ice and fresh-caught fish. And he'll kiss my neck with a hot mouth and tug on my hair with his fish-gut hands. They'll streak watery blood all over the dress and the sweetheart neckline that has fallen down to my navel, and I'll grip his spikes tight in my fists. He'll fuck me so hard, I'll lose one of my mother's clip-ons and underneath me a red heel will snap. And I'll stagger from the truck, earring-less and one heeled, to where my mother and Tom are waiting for me at an elegant oyster bar down the way.

Clutching the blood-strewn bag she bought me by its rhinestone handle. Fish guts in my hair. Blood and ice running in pink rivulets down my biceps, but I'll be grinning from ear to ear. I'll be grinning so hard its hurts my face.

I'll make a pit stop at the flower stall to watch them arrange stargazers. To the Vietnamese woman, I'll say, A bouquet, please. For my mother. I'll hold the stems in dangerously loose fingers, dragging their heads along the sidewalk. At the pier's edge, where she's watched me eat how many apples, where the homeless sleep curled on benches and the corporate men eat their gourmet grilled cheeses with their ties blowing backward in the breeze of the sound, I'll lie on the wet grass, the flowers across my lap, the yellow pollen spilling onto the white and black taffeta. Such gorgeous detail—look at the details, said my mother, taking the hem between her thumb and forefinger. Eating my apple, I'll smile at my own bruised legs splayed out in front of me, letting the juice run out of my mouth corners, and I'll look neither to the right nor to the left, but only at the light dancing on the gray water. And the taste of the apple, cold and sweet, will be like roses, will blend with the blood and salt and fish in my mouth, into something heavenly.

What the hell happened to you? my mother will say when I hand her the stargazers.

Fell, I'll tell her.

"Can I help you?" one of them says to me now.

"Help me?"

"Something you want from out of here?" he says, smacking the glass case with his rubber-gloved fist.

I look from the men back down to the display of splayed

fish. "That one," I say to him, pointing to it. Bigger than the last one. I smile at the curved teeth in its large open mouth, the gray-white tongue lolling out a little, silvery black scales broken along the sides of its beautifully hideous face.

"What, no four ounces today?"

"That's it. Thanks."

As I walk away, I realize that even though I was standing there for so long, not one drop of blood has touched me. Not even a bit of pinky water. When I turn away to go back to the restaurant, I don't even smell of fish, despite the package in my purse. I smell of apple and the Angel she dabbed in my neck hollows.

As I approach the table, I reach for my mother's glass of cava and nearly collapse into the oysters on ice, but he catches me with a firm grip.

"Careful there," Tom mumbles.

"Where did you disappear to?" my mother asks me.

"I told you. Toilet," I say, falling back into my chair. Even seated, I'm spinning. Through the floor-to-ceiling windows, I feel the tug of the dark water. I stare at the side of his face, hoping he'll turn toward me, steady me, but he keeps his gaze focused on my mother, the window, some distant point I can't fathom. I paw through my purse for a lighter, while the floor opens up beside me.

"Thought you'd fallen down it, didn't we?" my mother says, looking at Tom, who smiles politely. She reaches across the table and holds a tea light up to my unlit tip.

"We did," Tom says, taking my hand, not looking at me.

Later, he offers to take a picture of us with my mother's disposable while there's still some light in the sky.

"Could you?" she says.

"Okay, now lean in. A little closer together so I can get you both in." But no matter how close together he brings us with his hands, my mother and I still don't touch.

"He's a keeper," my mother says to me while she watches me pack Sunday morning. All the satiny strappy shoes I'll never wear again. Clothes that will ring wrong against my skin in terms of texture, in terms of color, the minute she isn't there to tap her toes and clap for me, like the sight of me is music, is the song she loves best. After we're done, we go to her balcony and have coffee, sit amid the dead stargazers in their stale green water. Through her sliding glass door that looks into the living room, we stare at his sleeping body curled on her sofa bed like we stared at the chimps at the zoo earlier this week. "Hang on to him," she says.

"I will," I say. Last night, after she went to bed, I reached for him and he turned away from me. I lay there awake beside him, watching the silent rise and fall of his body, listening to her gasp for breath in the next room. I thought of me in her ideas of sexy pressed up against a wall full of hooks. Making him destroy all the bits of gauze and lace with his hands and his lips until I'm a thing just peeled and blazing. And he either doesn't mind or doesn't see the traces of the girl I was before. Doesn't mind or doesn't see the raised skin and the slack skin. He doesn't see because we're in the dark of the truck or he doesn't care. He says the word *sexy* into the whorl of my ear like it's a live thing, a freshly shucked pearl. A secret I've pulled out of him in spite of himself, like sweet deep water from a well.

"He almost didn't recognize you, I'll bet," my mother says now, fishing.

What are you wearing anyway? That a new dress? he asked me later that night, when we were alone on my mother's balcony. I was smoking and he was staring out at the lake, keeping me company.

You don't like it?

I like it. Just I've never seen you in anything like it. It's . . . intense. He smiled. *It just doesn't really look like you, that's all.*

I looked at him looking at the water. *I can change,* I said.

Don't change. Why would you change?

I could feel myself start to cry, so I turned away and looked at the lake too. Tom reached over and took my cigarette from me. He inhaled shallowly, like a nonsmoker, coughing a little, holding it wrong.

When I was a kid, he said, *my dad would take me to the barber every four weeks and force me to get this buzz cut like he had in the air force. I hated it so much and finally one day, I told him. Dad, I hate this.*

What happened?

Tom took another drag of the cigarette. *He called me an asshole. Right there in front of the barber and all these old men getting their hair cut.*

What? But you were just a kid. I looked at his sandy hair, chin length and unbrushed.

That was my dad. He took one more drag, coughed and handed it back. *It's a nice color on you. It really is.*

"Almost," I tell my mother now. She watches me fold the last of my dresses into my suitcase. "What is it?" I ask her.

"Nothing," she says, watching me snap the suitcase shut. She helps herself to a croissant. "You'll call when you get home?"

"Yes." I won't. Not for a long time.

I watch her break the croissant in half, pick at each half until it's flakes, then eat it like it's dust. "Mom? Is there anything I should know?"

My mother looks down, begins to gather crumbs by pressing the pads of her fingers into the plate.

"About what?"

How you can't breathe, for a start. How you can't feel your feet. "About you," I say.

"Me?" My mother shrugs. Shakes her head. Refolds her arms on the table. I notice that underneath her linen coverall, she's wearing the same shapeless black shift dress she's been wearing almost every day since I got here. Stained with the sauce from last night's mussels. Her feet are still encased in the withered Keds. The only thing she's varied from day to day is a bolero of black lace and her costume jewelry. The violet set, made of blown Italian glass, lies in a small heap on the place mat. She looks shorn without it. With her spikes yet to be slicked, her hair looks shaggy around her face and lighter, almost auburn. She licks the rose petal jam quickly off the butter knife, presses the pads of her fingers into her plate to gather more crumbs but there are none.

Years after she dies, when I'm on vacation in a small seaside town, I will think I see her in an outdoor café. A woman in black wearing Jackie O sunglasses. She'll look exactly like my mother except she'll be thin. Seated alone at a table for two. I'll watch the afternoon sun lick her black hair red for I don't know how long, her nose tilted into an open book. Elegant sips of espresso, each one leaving a plummy lipstick imprint on the china. Ignoring a chocolate torte right in front of her. I'll look at her with my mouth open and tears in my eyes until she'll suddenly get up and leave. I'll follow her from the café to a butcher shop and then to a flower shop and then to a market and that's where I'll lose her. I'll turn circles in the midst of the stalls for what seems like hours before giving up and walking back to my hotel.

"Just you're beautiful," she says now to the empty plate. "Just I'll miss you." She reaches out, runs a hand along the side of my face, brushing a lock of hair back from my eyes. She tucks it behind my ear. There.

Fit4U

She took the dry cleaning ticket from me and disappeared behind the plastic shrouded coats and yellowed wedding dresses I don't know how long ago. I'm standing by the counter, smoking in her gutted aquarium of an establishment, trying not to breathe in the scent of chemicals and old clothes people should have thrown out, given away, maybe burned a long time ago. I'm feigning interest in the ugly walls, the dubious certificates, waiting for whatever it is my mother brought here a few days ago and never picked up.

I found the dry cleaning stub in her knockoff Gucci purse, which I picked up from the police station. It was in the swampy main pocket along with some loose change, one Chanel lipstick, and a worn leather wallet full of cards. The ticket was carefully folded, its corners nicked here and there with her uncapped plummy lipstick. *Fit4U,* the ticket says. *Pick up after 5:30 Mon to Fri. Pick up 2:30 Sat.* There's an address and a number underneath stamped in red ink.

I found Fit4U in a mini-mall on the outskirts of town, between a holistic center that looked closed and a Thai massage parlor that looked very open. A narrow storefront of murky glass. A small statue of a fat Buddha leering through the barred windows beside a profusely flowering fake plant. A woman behind the counter with hair and eye shadow out of John Waters, a worn tape measure around her neck. Glasses perched so far down the bridge of her slender nose, I wonder how she can possibly see out of them. She was wearing a sweater patterned with Christmas trees even though it was June. Her palms were pressed hard into the countertop like there could be a shotgun beneath it. There was a man sitting absolutely still on the rust-colored love seat beside the counter with his eyes wide open. Maybe she'd killed him. This is what I sincerely thought until I saw him blink.

Surely my mother did not come here, I thought, for her dry cleaning/alteration needs. Surely there was somewhere nicer she could have gone. I looked at the dry cleaning ticket again and sure enough, this was the address, and when I handed the woman behind the counter the stub, she didn't blink, just turned around and disappeared into the back of the store.

That was at least an hour ago now. Since then, I've taken a hungover tour of the mini-mall. Smoked five and a half cigarettes in my mother's Taurus with the window rolled down slightly, staring at the barred storefront through her streaked windshield, the scratched-off letters in the shirts/laundry/alterations sign, trying to think about nothing. Not the funeral director's message on my voice mail, his tone striving for grandfatherly. Telling me it's ready for me to pick up anytime. *It* meaning my mother.

Then I go back inside the shop, but she's still nowhere to be seen.

I stand at the counter, tapping my foot, my eyes fixed on a dusty bell beside the ancient cash register. An almost irresistible urge to ring that bell creeps into my fingers. "Hello?" I call out.

My cell phone starts ringing. Maybe my husband wondering where I am, or else the funeral director again. Yesterday, I sat across from this man at a highly polished table, staring at the gold rings on each of his swollen pinkies as he explained the cremation procedure, his voice that time attempting to emulate an ocean wave, the serenity that is eternal slumber. I focused my eyes on his rings so I wouldn't be blown apart by his words. I even felt myself nodding. Like yes, yes, I was interested, scientifically, in the combustion process, in how my mother would blow up in a box. How some of the ashes gathered might not be my mother's. But all of the ashes gathered would be mine to keep, of course. In a receptacle of my choosing. *We have several models to choose from, all quite tasteful, I think you'll find. Here.* And he slid a glossy catalog full of eyesores across the table for me to peruse. My task now to retrieve the least offensive of the ill-fitting options. I was used to hunting for that. So was my mother.

I let my phone ring.

"Hello?" I call again into the bowels of the shop.

No answer, no movement from inside the fortress of hanging clothes, not even a blink from the love seat man.

I ring the bell by the cash register. Nothing. I ring it again, harder.

"Jesus," the woman says, at last emerging from the back, and I realize I've been pounding on the bell for some time. I stop mid-bang, my palm still raised over the bell like it could strike again anytime.

"You her daughter?"

"Yes."

She gives me an appraising look but I'm in a black hole of a dress today, one in which you can't discern tit from waist from hip.

I see she's toting a dark dress shrouded in plastic by her finger crook. She's holding it at a distance, at arm's length, like I once saw a Mormon receptionist carry a cup of black coffee to her boss at an office I temped at. She hangs it up now on the chrome rack between us. Even before she does this, I recognize the dress. Deep blue like the hour between the dog and the wolf. An attractively scooped neckline. Sleeves and hemline a length and cut you would call kind. Buttons in back like discreetly sealed lips. Good give in the fabric. Double lined. The sort of dress that looks like nothing but a sad dark sack on the hanger, but on the body it's a different story. Takes extremely well to accessories. My mother loved this sort of dress. At whatever weight she was—thin, fat, middling— she owned an iteration. I saw her wear it to work, lunch with friends, on dates, to movies, parties, funerals. I saw her wear it alone in her apartment for days on end. Scratch at a stain on the boob. *Shit.* The hemline begin to unravel. *Fuck fuck fuck. Do you have a safety pin?* Holes begin to appear in the armpits. *Jesus.* The sleeves fray. *Well. That's that, isn't it?* She wore it so much she'd wear it out and then she'd have to hunt for another, whip through the plus-size racks for something that fit just as impossibly well, that was just as dignified, just as forgiving in its plain dark elegance.

I look at it now hanging in plastic on the rack. Whatever desire I have to cry dies when I see a note on a yellow square of paper safety-pinned to the neckline with some red loopy hand-writing on it. I've seen that yellow paper safety-pinned on this dress or one of its sisters before. Suddenly I'm business. My mother's hands pointing to the note, wanting answers, please.

"What's this?"

She sighs. Takes the dress off the hanger and spreads it on the counter between us. The smell of her perfume, her old sweat rises up ripe between us. There is my mother. Barefoot in her apartment, playing solitaire on her deck, splayed knees stretching the skirt, toes twiddling under the table. Lying on the sagging boat of her brass bed after a long workday, flipping channels, too tired to change. Asleep with her mouth open, her troubled breathing, the hemline hitched up and tangled around her legs.

She smooths down the fabric now, lifts up the hemline, exposing the myriad holes in the slip.

Seeing my face, she says, "Those she didn't even ask me to touch. You can't even see those. But I did raise the lining hem for her again, see?"

Fuck fuck fuck. Safety pin, do you have one?

"This, though." She points to a jagged hole on the hip.

Jesus.

"I couldn't fix this because it's not on the seam, see?" Then she pokes her finger through the hole and wags it back and forth, shaking her head.

Stop that! My mother's anger rising in my throat. Her hands itching through mine to take a swipe at this woman's wagging finger. "I see."

I watch her run her fingers along the frayed sleeves, the sagging neckline, the holes in the armpits, all lost causes according to her.

"Nothing you can do about that," she says each time she points to a rip, a fray, a hole, raising her chin to look at me through her narrow little frames. "I told her."

I nod, a heady mix of rage and shame spreading through my chest like fire.

"Now, here." She turns the dress around and shows me the back.

I look at the new black buttons she's sewn down the spine. There are only two of the original buttons left at the base, small, dainty iridescent bulbs like pearls. "I told her I might not have something like these," she says, waggling the two pearly ones like they were dubious anyway, fanciful.

"Don't touch those." The words come out of my mouth like a cough, my mother's low growl suffusing my own hiss.

"Excuse me?"

I stare at the buttonholes, worn from all the give and tug they've endured. I see the expanse of my mother's back, the red imprints of zippers and too-tight buttons on her skin along the spine.

Can you button this for me?

Giving me her back and putting her hands up in the air like she was being arrested.

You can't do it, she'd say after a while, her raised arms beginning to sag downward, her spine going slack.

Hang on, I'd say.

Okay I'll stop breathing. Here. Try now.

"But here's the real problem," the woman continues. She points to a small cluster of holes by the hip that look like the dress was gored on one side by Freddy Krueger. "I mean, what even happened here?" There's accusation in her voice.

The rage in me dies abruptly, momentarily.

"I don't know."

"Well." she says, pushing the dress across the counter toward me, "Nothing I can do about it."

"What do you mean *nothing*?" I push the dress across the counter toward the woman. "Surely something?" I add in a quieter voice, one that sounds like my own.

"Nothing," she says, shoving the dress back at me.

"Nothing." The word falls from my lips like a stone.

And that's when it comes back to me in stereo: mothers of various sizes, mothers of varying hairstyles—permed in the eighties, waved and wispy-banged in the nineties, choppy in her final years—but always the same plummy mouth twisted, the same face contorted by outrage and shame, storming out of glass doors with the same broken, balled-up dark dress in her fist. Tossing it into the backseat of the car and slamming the door with a violence that always made me jump. Screeching out of the parking lot while the seamstress behind the counter within, always with the same tape measure around her neck, the same glasses on the far end of her nose, either watched through the window or didn't. My mother driving without a seat belt all the way home, the car making a little dinging noise she ignored.

Nothing, all these versions of my mother told me when I asked what happened, shaking their heads, their fingers frantically turning the radio dial for a song, any song, to fill the car.

My cell phone starts ringing again. Or maybe it's been ringing this whole time.

"Go try another place," the woman's saying now. "They'll tell you the same thing I'm telling you." She's looking at me as if daring me to accuse her again.

I could snatch the dress the off the counter and head to the door like I actually have another place to go. Can see my mother looking at her, poised for more fighting, or maybe at this point she'd be ready to give it up.

Well. That's that, isn't it?

I nod. Suddenly I feel very tired. Like I could sleep for a hundred years.

"Look, I won't charge you for the hemline repair, just the cleaning, okay?" She says it more softly now.

"Okay." But we both know the dress is beyond cleaning. Even before this woman removed the plastic, it smelled pungently of my mother. I watch her put the plastic covering back on.

"Tell her I tried, okay? But maybe not to bring this one back in again."

Good choice, the funeral director said when at last I pointed to one of the vessels at random. *Elegant. Tasteful. And who doesn't love blue?*

She takes it off the rack and into her arms, gently now, like it's a maiden, Snow White fresh from her glass coffin. There is such great care in the gesture that it brings another mother back to me briefly. One I didn't see very much. Happy. At ease in her flesh. "I'll tell her," I say.

She'll Do Anything

They're finishing off their second round of drinks when Dickie starts wanting to tell them about this fat chick he's been banging lately. Being Dickie, he doesn't mind going into detail. How her tits clap when he's taking her from behind. How you'd assume—he'd assumed, anyway—that she would be, you know, loose down there, but actually, surprise, surprise. "Gastro sex," Dickie says, draining his Fireball. "Best sex I've ever had, hands down."

"She has this big scar down her stomach from this gastric bypass she had, like, a year ago," Dickie says. He leans back from the bar and traces a line down his own shiny shirtfront with his long, slender fingers. "Guess it didn't work though or something because she's still—"

"For fuck's sake, Dickie," Tom says, "I'm *eating*." He stares down at his untouched mound of stale chips covered in half-melted Monterey Jack. The only thing grimmer than the Macho Nacho platter at the Dead Goat is the fact that he himself engineered the software that ensures its efficient expedition from the kitchen. Tom looks at Hot Pocket for reinforcement—he is, after all, their supervisor of sorts—but Hot Pocket is grinning at Dickie over the rim of the shot he's about to take, saying, "You're a sick man, Dick." It's so Dickie, these antics. Like the time he told them all about how he bought a rubber vagina and then returned it a week later—all banged up and soggy with baby oil—making a big stink in the sex store about how the pubes "didn't ring true." Dickie has a unique ability to forage deep into the peripheries of the perverse and come back, polo shirt collar popped and grinning like a guy in a beer commercial, like life is just one big, hilarious frat boy stunt.

Hot Pocket announces they're going to need another round for this, even though he's too drunk to drive and has one DUI already. He signals to their waitress.

"So how fat are we talking anyway?" Hot Pocket says.

Dickie appears to consider the question. Considering it, Tom thinks, like it's a philosophical quandary. What is the sound of one hand clapping?

"Not like those chicks on the birthday cards that say, 'Pick a Fold and Fuck It,'" he says at last, "but, you know, decent."

"That's disgusting," Hot Pocket says.

"Sure, the belly's not so hot." Dickie shrugs with the air of a cult leader, above the understanding of the masses. "But I think pounding away at that ass might be curing me of PUP." PUP is Dickie's shorthand for Potentially Unable to Perform.

"Anyway, the best thing about fucking her?" Dickie continues, ignoring Tom's dark look. "She'll do anything."

Tom gazes at Dickie from across the table, sitting contentedly under the antlered shadow of a goat skull on the wall. "What do you mean she'll do anything?"

"I mean anything," Dickie says, smiling.

They fall silent while their waitress approaches the table and sets down their drinks.

"I fucked Judy once," Hot Pocket confesses quietly, after the waitress has left. He is referring to the plump, sad woman in IT who is in every way the physical opposite of Brindy, his ex-stripper-turned-freelance-interior-decorator wife, for whom he recently purchased breast implants.

"Judy doesn't count," says Dickie, like he's a connoisseur of such things.

"What do you mean Judy *doesn't count*?"

"What's Judy, like, a size 12? I'm talking about an actual fat girl."

"Jesus, keep it down," Tom says, eyeing the group of waitresses behind the bar giving each other *Can you believe him?* looks.

"Don't knock it till you've *actually* tried it is all I'm saying," Dickie says. "In fact, you guys should. I'm sure she'd be up for it. She's a real trooper, like I said."

"Think I'll pass," Hot Pocket says.

"Don't know what you're missing. Tom knows what I'm talking about. Or he did anyway—right, Tom?"

"No idea," Tom says, though his eyes say, *Little prick.*

Zigzagging down the interstate, Tom mutters *sick fuck* and *little prick* to the windshield. Between the summer storm and the shots, he can barely see the broken yellow line dividing the lanes, but thanks to Dickie, he can see the ass of the fat girl clear as a full moon on a winter night.

Tom lives with his wife in an apartment complex he hates just off the highway. On top of it being largely filled with douche-bag executives, he got tricked into paying ninety-five extra dollars a month for what he was told would be a mountain view but what is in fact only a sliver of the foothills eclipsed by the gawdy lights of the steak house across the street. Normally he would never agree to live in the sort of place that gives you a complimentary Frappuccino and a biscotti upon signing your lease, but Beth no, *Elizabeth*— he must remember she wants to be called Elizabeth now—was keen because it was one of the few complexes in town with a fitness center. That two dusty treadmills, a StairMaster that makes the sound of a dying coyote when you step on it, and a rack of ancient weights were what stood between him and a nice floor of a house somewhere is something he still finds difficult to accept. "Just because you don't want to drive *five* minutes to Gold's Gym down the road, I'm supposed to *live* with a bunch of assholes?" is what he wanted to say, but didn't because he was being supportive.

He comes home to find Beth in the kitchen, surrounded by little piles of julienned vegetables, angrily grating jicama on a mandolin. She is wearing a dark, very tight cocktail dress. Probably new. Purchased during her break at work or perhaps online at night. A few months after she reached her goal and hit what she called a plateau, she started buying these sorts of dresses with an alarming greed and regularity. He is convinced she would devour them, these dark, tailored dresses, if she could, like the chips or ice cream she allows herself once every two weeks. Seeing her in one now still makes him think she'll want to go out somewhere, but he's starting to get used to the fact that this is just how she dresses now. Always. Am I overdressed? she always asks. Yes, he wants to say. You look great, is what he says. Does she look great? She does. Of course she does—look at her. She is a sleek, beautiful young woman, younger looking even than her twenty-eight years, except maybe around the eyes. Even though he himself has borne witness to her transformation over the past three years, he is still getting used to the severely pared-down point of her chin, the now visible web of bones in her throat, how all the once-soft edges of her have suddenly grown knife sharp. How they seem pointed at him in perpetual, quiet accusation.

Like it has been every night for more than a year now, the kitchen is thick with the scent of boiled barn and burnt vegetable, like Mother Nature on fire.

"Something smells good, Beth," he says, in the overly jolly voice he speaks in when he's been hanging around Hot Pocket all day.

She looks at him.

"What?"

"I told you not to call me that anymore, remember?"

"Sorry." He puts his hands up like she's holding a gun. "Something smells good, Elizabeth."

"Nearly ready," she says. She pulls out of the oven a tray of what looks to him like burnt turds. Every night, she sullenly exercises this form of torture upon a green in the cabbage family. It used to be she would offer to make things for him—ham and cheese scones, potato leek soup—on top of whatever punishing concoctions of grain, bean curd, and sprout she'd cooked up for herself. Recently, though, she's been on what she calls "a slippery slope." He doesn't know what this means, exactly, but he promised to "be more supportive."

"Looks great," he murmurs now, watching her pile a maggotylooking grain that smells like hoof onto his plate. He pokes tentatively at the mound with the tines of his fork.

"What are these little wormy things called again?"

"Quinoa."

"What-wa?"

She takes a sip of Chilean white, which she first poured in a measuring cup before pouring it into a glass, and watches him push the larval beads around with his fork. "I could just make you a grilled cheese," she says.

"I eat what you eat, remember? That another new dress?"

"This? Yes."

"Looks good."

"You think so? It isn't too much?"

He gazes at the odd bows on the sleeves, the asymmetrical neckline, the thin little belt around the severely tailored middle.

"Um, too much how?"

"I don't know. Too tight?"

He looks at her sitting eerily straight opposite him. It is so extraordinarily tight that she has to sit rigid in her chair.

"No." And he quickly shoves in a forkful of the larvae. The face he makes when he swallows happens without him meaning it to.

"Jesus, Tom. Let me just make the sandwich, okay?"

"No, this is interesting. Really." He takes another bite, this time quickly chasing it with the Fat Tire he brought to the table.

She snorts something into her wine.

"What was that?"

"Nothing. So how was work anyway?"

He takes a swig of his Fat Tire. Back when she used to visit him in her heavier days, she was content to enjoy dinner in what he thought was an amicable silence, smoking a Camel Light while he slurped takeout in front of an old monster movie. Now that they eat boiled grains over candlelight, she demands dinner conversation. As he yammers on about various parts of his day, often trailing off, only to be prompted by a clipped *What else?* he feels like one of those old mechanical toy puppies being forced to do flips.

It's after her third *What else?* that he ends up telling her about Dickie's foray into gastro sex. "He even offered her to us. Hot Pocket and me. Isn't that sick?"

"Why are you telling me this?"

"Just thought you would find it funny," he says, taking another swig of his Fat Tire.

He didn't mean to mention that last bit about the offer, but now it's out there. He can't take it back. He watches her grow eerily quiet as she chews on this new bit of knowledge along with a mouthful of sprouts.

"I don't know," she says at last, lighting a cigarette and tipping ash into her plate. "Maybe you should take him up on it."

"Beth."

"It could be fun for you. Nostalgic."

He sighs, picks a small yellow ball out of the wilted pile of California greens that comprise the side salad. He turns it around in his fingers, squinting at it like it's a miniature globe, like it contains the whole world.

"What is this anyway, a kumquat?"

What he intended was simply to change the trajectory of the conversation. Instead, her face, or what's left of it, becomes a throbbing red blotch. "*No.*"

"Huh," he says, turning it around once more. "Looks like one."

"Well it fucking *isn't*, okay?"

"Jesus. Get a grip. It's not a kumquat. Got it. Sorry I'm not a genius chef like some people."

He thinks she'll laugh, but instead tears fill her eyes.

"What's wrong?"

"Nothing."

He sighs, sips his Fat Tire, lets her cry for a while, his eyes on the thin white Doric pillar to the left of her. It's the most pointless pillar in the whole world, he thinks, eyeing it. It holds nothing up. It stands there, cutting off the living room from the dining room, because it is the kind of crap that impresses the kind of schmucks who go in for an apartment with free biscotti and a fitness center. She's strung some purple Christmas lights around it she never turns on, which only adds to its absurdity.

"I just hate how you see me is all," she says, swatting the tears away like flies, but it's no good—they keep coming, causing her chin arrow to quiver pitifully.

"What do you mean how do I see you?" He looks at her intently, soberly through a dense and rippling puddle of drunk; she immediately lowers her eyes and turns her head, obscuring her face with a curtain of long black hair, a defensive gesture left over from her heavier days.

"I don't know," she says, pretending to examine her nails. "As some fucking . . . you know . . . *kumquat* eater."

"That's ridiculous," he says. "You're being ridiculous."

She rises from the table. He hears a lot of cupboard and fridge door slamming, the glugging sound of her pouring more wine into her measuring cup, then pouring it into a glass. She returns with a glass of what looks like another two ounces of white and, her evening ritual, a square of dark chocolate from a bar she keeps at the back of the cupboard like an alcoholic's hidden stash of gin. Seeing her huddled over this small square is sadder to him than the vegetable turds or the larval grains or the carefully measured glasses of bone-dry white. It's like watching a woeful squirrel hunched over a piece of trash he has mistaken for a winter nut.

"You'd like to, wouldn't you?" she says quietly, after what feels like an interminable silence.

"Like to what?" he asks, knowing exactly, but he wants to hear her say it.

"Nothing," she says.

"No, tell me, *Elizabeth*. What would I like?" He looks at her but she keeps her eyes on her ashed-up plate.

"To fuck that fat girl."

Jesus. He did push her to say it but he still can't believe she's said it out loud. It feels like a slap. He leaves with a mild slam of the door, even though she calls his name twice to come back.

In the empty parking lot outside Del Taco, he sits in his Honda and drinks his super-size Coke, shoving damp chili fries into his mouth gluttonously, staring neither at the bug-streaked wind-shield nor at the starless night but straight ahead. Back when Beth first lost the weight, she used to treat herself to a biweekly plate of cheesy fries, which they'd get at a sit-down fast food place that had big fake leather booths with phones in them where you placed your order. She'd eat them with a mixture of ketchup and mayon-naise. Even though he grew up in the state where they invented this concoction, it grossed him out slightly, watching her greedily whip the red and white gloops together with a matchstick fry until they formed an obscene bloody pink. He even made a face once at the sight. She saw the face and cried. Didn't eat anything but her draconian fare in front of him for months afterward.

A call from Beth is making his cell vibrate on the passenger seat for the fourth time. He ignores it. When he gets home he'll tell her the phone fell between the seats.

When he gets back, she's curled on the couch, flipping through a cookbook called *Roast Chicken and Other Stories*, watching *America's Next Top Model*. The only thing more disturbing than when she does this is when she watches the Food Network with a legal pad on her lap, taking notes for decadent meals he knows she'll never make.

"Went for Wendy's, did we?" she says, not looking up from the screen.

"Course not." It isn't a lie.

He sits beside her on the couch. She's watching the final episode of cycle ten. He knows this because this is the one cycle she has on iTunes, the one she watches the most often, where a plus-size model wins. The first time they watched the fat girl win—he didn't so much watch as look up every now and then from playing *World of Warcraft* on his laptop—even he was moved. He thought, Good for her. Good for *society*. He turned to look at Beth thinking she would be ecstatic, and was surprised to see a punched-in look of abject pain on her face.

"Jesus, Beth. What is it?"

"I just think that Somalian girl should have won. She had prettier features. Overall."

Despite this stance, she still watches this episode every so often, always with a shameful fascination. When it's over, she turns off the TV, closes *Roast Chicken and Other Stories*, and looks at him.

"Are you coming to bed?"

"In a bit. Think I'll just fuck around on the computer for a while first."

Dickie won't shut up about the fat girl. Tom figured after a few weeks, Dickie would have moved on to other pastures. That once more, he'd start telling tales about a hot receptionist's subpar blowing technique or how he got one of the Goldman Sachs girls who work nearby drunk enough on Tito's to dress up as a furry. But no, every time Dickie opens his mouth it's to tell them about this chick. How it's the best sex he's ever had. He can't even quite put it into words, it's so good. It's like they've reached a higher sexual plane or something. Really, it's enough to drive anyone crazy. He talks about it over Fireballs at Dead Goat. Pizza benders at the Italian Village. The free lunch buffet at the nearby strip bar, Southern X-posure, where Dickie's eyes don't even graze the firm curves of the glaring dancers whom he describes as hot but dead inside. Over cigarettes in the office parking lot, the exhaust from the nearby interstate blowing in their faces like an end-of-the-world wind, Dickie tells them it's getting serious. In fact, he thinks he might be in love. Last night, he's pretty sure they broke some records. After, they got high and made butter tartlets. He brings in a Tupperware container full of them and offers some to the fat secretaries, all of whom snatch greedy handfuls and say they're just scrumptious. "Aren't they, though?" Dickie winks.

He offers one to Tom, who coldly refuses.

Saturday. Fourth of July. He and Beth are driving toward Hot Pocket's house for the staff barbecue. She's sulking in the passenger's seat, hunched over a veggie platter with a ramekin of fat-free hummus in the center. Hunched as much as she can be, given that she is wearing yet another far-too-tight dress. New. Black, like she's in mourning. Patterned with small, prim flesh-colored flowers. Fishnets. Heels. To a barbecue.

"Is it too much?" she asked him on their way out the door.

My god, yes.

"You look great."

Now she isn't talking to him, just staring fixedly at the windshield. When he asks her what she wants to listen to, she says, "Whatever you'd like." He pats her knee and she pats his hand but she's still staring at the windshield.

"Seriously, you choose," she says to the glass. Probably she's upset because she's missing what she calls her "treat day." Every other Saturday night, she permits herself two double margaritas and enchiladas verdes at the Blue Iguana, followed by a Brownie Bonanza at Ben & Jerry's. Though it scares and saddens him a little to see her hunger let loose upon a small complimentary basket of tortilla chips, he too looks forward to these Saturday nights. It's the only night when her smirk goes slack, the noose of restraint loosened enough for her features to soften, her beauty at last unbuckling its belt. She is never more expansive and easygoing in conversation than when she's snatching chips from the basket with quick fingers. He's learned not to look at the fingers. If he does, she'll stop. On those nights, they discuss what they used to discuss on those long phone chats and during her first visits: movies and books and their mutual music loves and hates. It's good for a while. What he does not relish is seeing the naked disappointment splayed across her face when the last chip has been eaten, the final spoon of ice cream swallowed, the knowledge that there is another two weeks of sprouts ahead dimming her features like a pre-storm sky. And then of course, on the way home, she'll begin to feel sick. *I'm so full. I shouldn't have done it. I didn't even enjoy it. Do we have any Perrier at home?* She'll spend the rest of the evening scowling and sucking back Perriers from the bottle, too full and sick for sex.

"Hot Pocket'll have chips and salsa there," he tells her now. "Ice cream too. All that fun stuff." He tries to pat her knee again, but she moves away.

She readjusts the jicama and fennel batons on her vegetable tray. Who puts jicama batons on a vegetable tray? He can picture some bleach-toothed Food Network chef saying to the camera, "A vegetable tray doesn't have to be *all* carrots, celery, and grape tomatoes! Why not raise the *wow factor* by adding jicama, fennel, spring onions?" He can see Beth curled on the couch, nodding in agreement, jotting it down on her legal pad to try later, along with all the other kumquat-like items he can never identify that his life is suddenly full of, funking up his fridge and making all the bones inside his wife more visible.

"I can't eat there," she says now.

"Why not?"

"You *know* why not."

The rain's coming down again, but it's one of those brief, intense showers they often get in summer.

"No, I really don't."

"I can't eat in front of *her*."

By *her*, she means Brindy, the ex-stripper Hot Pocket's married to. Ever since that one time Tom let his eyes linger a little too long on her cleavage as she offered him pigs in a blanket from a tray, Beth has had it in for her.

"Do you think they'll be okay barbecuing this?" she says suddenly, holding up a soggy Yves veggie burger in a plastic bag.

Tom winces at the sight of the fake grill marks, the sad little kernels of corn and pea poking out of the damp taupe patty.

"Don't see why not."

"Well, I wouldn't want to offend Brindy. Can we listen to something a bit less depressing?"

"You don't like this? It's yours. I found it in your collection." He'd put on an old Dead Can Dance album she used to listen to on near continuous loop when he first met her. She would lie there while it played, looking up at the ceiling completely still, like she was dead.

Now she's looking at the car speaker as though it is a spider she wants dead but is too afraid to kill. He turns off the music. "What do you want to listen to, then?"

"Whatever you want. Just nothing *too* amped up. And nothing too depressing." That's code for electronica, classical, and pretty much everything else he loves that she used to love too.

"This isn't depressing. It's just sad. Sad is beautiful. Sad makes me happy."

"Well, it just makes me sad."

He looks at her rearranging her shawl across her thin shoulders. This woman who, on their first visits, used to love nothing more than lying on her back on his hardwood floor, content to let tears drip from her eye corners and pool in her ears for whole Nick Cave albums.

"Her tits are fake, you know," she says now. "Brindy's tits." She never ceases to remind him of this.

"So I've heard," he says.

"Also they leak. She told me herself. She's had to have, like, a million surgeries to correct it. Because they leak. It's sad, really."

"It is," he says, eyes on the road. "Very sad."

Brindy answers the door in cutoff jean shorts and a sleeveless T-shirt, an outfit that Beth will later tell him she wore on purpose to taunt her.

"Tom!" Brindy cries, giving him a hug.

"I hardly recognized you, Elizabeth," she says, smiling at her. Provoking her, Beth would say. "You look beautiful. You're always so dressed up, I love it."

And can you believe when she made that comment about she loved how dressed up I was? she will say later. *I mean, my god. What a vajazzled cunt.*

In Beth's dark glare, Tom is careful, supremely careful not to let his eye dwell too long on the long supple legs, the firm breasts of his buddy's wife.

In the kitchen, Brindy offers them both watermelon daiquiris. "You have to try them. They're *so* yummy!" In his peripheral vision, he sees Beth's face darken, becoming an abacus of sugar and carb counting. Unable to watch, he leaves them there in the kitchen before he can hear her ask, Do you have any dry white?

Outside, Hot Pocket is flipping T-bones on the barbecue in his Oakleys, a pyramid of marinated beef on a large aluminum platter to his left. Ribs. Tenderloins. More T-bones. He's wearing Bermuda shorts and one of those T-shirts that says GAME OVER featuring an altar-bound bride and groom standing side by side, the groom with little X's in his eyes.

"Tom," he says, fishing a Fat Tire out of the cooler and tossing it over.

"We, uh, brought something for the grill," Tom says, holding up the soggy packet of veggie patty like it's the tail of a dead skunk.

"Jesus." Hot Pocket raises his Oakleys and holds the package up to the sunlight. "What the hell is this anyway?"

Tom shrugs. "Some sort of tofu thing. It's for Beth," he adds, in a slightly lowered voice.

Hot Pocket looks over at Beth, who is scowling between two tiki torches, sniffing doubtfully at a blue corn chip. Tom wants Hot Pocket to protest this addition to the barbecue in the holy name of all this meat he's about to set fire to, but he just slaps him on the back and says, "Can do."

Tom stays hunched morosely by the meat smells, getting drunk on Fat Tires until his view of the backyard begins to sway a little. A few more people arrive. Most of the men, he sees, are looking at Beth, who is too busy glaring at Brindy to notice. He grabs another Fat Tire from the cooler.

"So where's Dickie anyway?" he mutters aloud. "Thought he was coming to this thing." All week Dickie had said he'd be coming. He even threatened to bring his new girlfriend.

"Yes," Brindy calls from the picnic table, "where is Dickie?" Everyone knows no party really starts until Dickie's arrived.

"Probably fucking that fat girl," Beth says, and by the way she says it, Tom knows she's at least two drinks past tallying up alcohol units and carbohydrate grams.

"What fat girl?" Brindy asks.

"Just this chick Dickie's dating right now," Hot Pocket says, giving the steaks another flip.

"Awww. I think that's sweet," Brindy says, grabbing a handful of corn chips.

"It is not *sweet*," Beth spits. "He calls it *gastro sex*, for God's sake. And he's only fucking her 'cause she'll do anything. How is that *sweet*?"

"*I* think it's sweet," Brindy insists quietly, nibbling on a corn chip.

"Not sure how I'm going to tell when this is done, Elizabeth," Hot Pocket says, poking at the veggie patty with his tongs. "These, uh, grill marks here are a little confusing."

"Just when it starts to get brown, Matt." She always calls him Matt. *Because I'm not calling a grown man Hot Pocket.*

"K," Hot Pocket says doubtfully. He slaps the patty on the grill. It starts to hiss and pop, like an evil, unending fart.

Tom had been looking forward to this meal of meat and corn on the cob and chips and mayonnaisey salads all week. But now that it's all piled before him beautifully on a paper plate, he can't eat. Instead he feels his blood pressure rise, his fork grip become tighter as he hears his wife say, No, No, No, but thanks, to nearly every dish offered. He relaxes a little when at last she accepts some garden salad to accompany her plate of jicama sticks and a bunless veggie patty. When she begins to stab lamely at the lettuce, he decides he's not going to let her ruin this for him any longer and tears into his ribs violently but without pleasure.

"How come you're not having any?" asks Maddy, the seven-year-old daughter of Hot Pocket and Brindy, addressing Beth. Maddy is dressed as a fairy princess and her mouth is covered in barbecue sauce. She's gazing at Beth intently with her mother's large hazel eyes.

Beth looks from Maddy's paper wings to her plastic tiara and gives her an awkward smile. "Because I don't eat meat."

"Maddy, honey, eat your burger," Brindy says.

But Maddy isn't interested in her burger. She is staring at Beth. Tom winces, hearing the child's question before the words even form on her barbecue sauce–stained lips.

"Didn't you used to be really f—"

"You know," Brindy interrupts, "I just love that dress, Elizabeth. Where did you say you got it again?"

He feels Beth looking at him from across the table, but keeps his gaze fixed on the half-gnawed ribs on his plate.

Tom and Hot Pocket are in the side yard, smoking a joint in the glare of a Japanese foot lantern. He can hear the drunken squawk of Brindy and Beth discussing flaxseed oil and inner thigh exercises. He sees she has even accepted a tiny glass of Brindy's watermelon daiquiri, her resentment having taken a reluctant backseat to her gratitude at being saved from a seven-year-old's bluntness.

"You're a lucky man, Tom," Hot Pocket tells him, slapping him on the back.

"Yeah," he mumbles. People keep telling him this. They look at Beth, Elizabeth, whatever the hell her name is now, at her long black hair and her smooth, fair skin and how what's left of her flesh is packaged so daintily into a neat, hot little dress and tell him this. But what Tom sees is the stooped-over way she carries herself like her thinness was a punch in the gut, the air of heaviness around her that will never leave. How her heels are scuffed and her stockings full of rips because she spends all her money on dresses that she cannot afford and that are not fit for any occasion. He has fantasies about burning the little short-sleeved black cardigan she feels compelled to wear even in the dead of summer, over this dress, over every dress regardless of its color and cut because she buys them all too tight. He's seen the deodorant stains in the armpits, smelled the stink of its sweat and trying and perfume. And he doesn't feel like a lucky man. He doesn't feel lucky at all.

For one thing, he got lucky a hell of a lot more when she was fat. Now she's either too hungry or angry or distracted for sex. Or she says she still feels "like a stranger in my own body." When she first told him this, he said it was ridiculous. But actually he understands what she means. He feels shy and awkward when he hugs the half of her that's left, when his hands graze the now pronounced bones in her back and shoulders. And she is just as uncomfortable being naked, obsessed with what she calls "the evidence." Embarrassed about her shrunken breasts, the slack skin around her middle. She still comes to bed more or less fully clothed and covering parts of herself with her hands, just like she did when she was fat.

The fat girl comes back to him like a remembered dream.

"Where the hell's Dickie, anyway?"

"Don't know."

"Can you believe he actually offered that girl to us?"

Hot Pocket laughs and takes a toke. "That's Dickie. He's a sicko."

He forgets if he's the first to suggest it or if it's Hot Pocket. How they ought to just drive over there. To Dickie's house. Not to . . . you know . . . obviously, but just to get a look at her. This fat chick. This girl who'll do anything. Just, you know, for curiosity's sake. Hot Pocket checks his watch. It's early still. He probably shouldn't leave the party.

"You said we need more beers," Tom says. "We could get more beers on the way."

"I guess we could." They do need more beers.

They tell the girls they're going out to get more beers and the next thing he knows he's driving across the tracks in Hot Pocket's

SUV, zigzagging past the rancid Mexican eateries and gang war gas stations in the no-man's-land between Hot Pocket's neighborhood and Dickie's. He is expecting Dickie to live in a glass cube or a giant dildo or something, but it's just a regular old bungalow. Sad and squat and flesh colored, just like all the other ones on the block.

The house looks dark. Though Tom's already charging across the lawn, Hot Pocket hangs back. "Wait," he calls. "It's getting pretty late, isn't it?"

"This is Dickie we're talking about," Tom replies. "His evening of hydro and samurai movies is probably just getting under way."

Despite Hot Pocket's protests, Tom staggers up the walk, rings the doorbell and gathers his hands together in front of him, rocks on his heels. His hands feel very moist and hot. No answer.

He pounds and pounds on the door until his knuckles are raw, ignoring Hot Pocket's *Let's just go*s, thinking he will never leave, not until he gets a look. At last Dickie appears bleary-eyed in the doorway. He's wearing one of those shirts patterned with dancing hula girls, unbuttoned down to the navel. There is a sedate, rumpled look to him, a sheen to his face that suggests he's just been masturbating.

"Hey, guys. What the fuck? Little late for a house call, isn't it?"

Over Hot Pocket's drunken apology Tom says, "Just were going for more beers and wanted to check up on you. Thought you and your date were coming to the party tonight."

"Oh." Dickie blinks. "That was tonight? Guess we got kind of caught up."

"So . . . ?" Tom says, craning his neck to catch a glimpse of the dark hallway behind Dickie.

"So what?" Dickie says, narrowing the gap in the doorway so only he is visible. Tom notices a darting, ferret-like quality in his eyes.

"Can we come in?" Tom asks, ignoring Hot Pocket's backward tug on his arm.

"*Now?*" Dickie says.

Tom shrugs. "Didn't know the Fourth of July was a school night. Anyway, we just wanted to see . . . to say hello."

Dickie looks hard at Tom, who looks hard back. He shakes his head. "Night, assholes," he says. He is about to close the door on them when Tom quickly slips his foot in the crack.

"What the fuck is wrong with you, Tom?"

Tom doesn't answer. Keeps his foot in the door, his eyes sifting the dark hall beyond Dickie's shoulder.

"Fuck off!"

That's when he hears a woman's voice from within: "Everything okay?"

"Everything's fine," Dickie calls, glaring at Tom.

Tom's gaze grasps for her shape in the dark but as far as he can see there's nothing. Her voice sounds nothing like Beth's. He looks back at Dickie, who's still scowling in his hula girl shirt. He feels Hot Pocket tugging his shoulder while offering mumbled entreaties that they should probably head home. Sighing, Tom removes his foot from the doorframe. The door slams in his face.

When they get back to the party, Brindy tells him Beth has already left. Not only didn't she stay for the fireworks, but also? "She seemed upset."

Driving home alone in Hot Pocket's SUV, Tom feels the

mountain ranges on either side of him, visible only as a darker blackness in the black.

Reeling through the apartment door, he calls her name a couple of times. No answer. But the living room pillar's there and she's lit it up. He walks toward it like it's a beacon, sees on the mantel of the fireplace all these photos of the new her—of her and him, her and her mother, some just of her, of Elizabeth—not his Beth but Elizabeth. Looking pared down and stiff, clad in tight-fitting, sharply cut dresses of every shade, her lips a hard red line that is only half-smiling on one side. In the center, the urn filled with her mother's ashes, which she refuses to scatter. As he turns and makes his way to the bedroom, he passes the workout gizmo she ordered off the Home Shopping Network, something between a NordicTrack and a treadmill, called the Gazelle. The Gazelle is for days, she said, when she doesn't feel like "facing" the fitness center, whatever that means. There are so many things he no longer understands.

There, between the display for calories burned and miles Gazelled, she's taped a photo of herself taken at the staff barbecue a couple of years ago, which she attended during one of her visits, when still in the process of losing. She's folded the picture in half so it's just her, but when he unfolds it, he sees himself, red faced and grinning noncommittally at the camera, one thin arm dangling around her shoulder. Beth is leaning into him, smiling broadly into his armpit, a big S of dark shiny hair obscuring one of her eyes. She's wearing a long black oversize sweater, a long dark skirt. My fat dress, she calls it now. That night, some asshole coworker's skeletal wife apparently took a cheap shot at her weight and he didn't defend her. At least this is what she claimed when they got home. He doesn't remember not defending her. He guesses she Gazelles about five miles a day now while looking at this half of the picture, in which she is smiling but also looking a little scared, like the camera could give her a clip to the jaw anytime. This was the girl he fell in love with. The girl who loved sad music, the girl who wanted nothing more than to lie with him in the dark and let wave upon wave of lush, dark electronic sound wash over her. This might be the only photo of her left. Maybe she keeps the others hidden in a box somewhere, but probably she just got rid of them.

I did this for you, you know, she always tells him.

Did you? he wants to say.

Because he doesn't remember ever asking for kumquats or hybrid cardio machines, but who knows? Maybe all this time, all the little ways he looked at her and didn't look at her, all the things he said or didn't say or didn't say enough added up to this awful request without his knowledge or consent, like those ransom notes made from letters cut from different magazines.

He takes the picture of Beth off the Gazelle, scratches the tape off the corners, and holds it up to the blinking purple lights. As he gazes at it, swaying a little from the beers and pot, his fingers itch to do something with it—set fire to it, put it in a frame. He's about to tear it up when he hears sex sounds, forced, violent, and oddly familiar, from down the hall.

He finds her sitting at the desk with his laptop open before her. Her back is to him, her bony shoulder blades pointed at him like arrows of accusation, the moans of all of his uncleared history boomeranging through the small, thin-walled room. It looks to him like the one he watched the other night about the two fat maids, specifically the scene in which they demonstrate their versatility to their employers. Only he doesn't remember it being this loud. In the window's reflection, he can see her hand covering her mouth, her expression frozen in horror and disgust and fascination.

"Beth," he calls like a question, but it's no good. He can see she is far too transfixed by the fat girls, by the spectacle of flesh which she Gazelled countless miles to shed, by the ecstasy which she is now too hungry and tired and angry to summon. And he knows that she must see him there in the window's reflection, standing in the dark doorway, softly calling her name.

The von Furstenberg and I

Despite my better judgment, I'm in the fitting room wrestling with the von Furstenberg again. I've thrown it over my head and I'm attempting to wedge my arms through the armholes even though it's got my shoulders and rib cage in a vise grip. The fabric's stretched tight over my face so I can't see and it's blocking my air supply but I'm doing my best to breathe through twill. This is the moment of deepest despair. This is the moment she always chooses to knock on the door.

I can hear the slow-approaching clicks of her heels. Three light raps on the door with her opal-encrusted knuckles. I brace myself for the sound of her voice, all of my nerve endings like cats ready to pounce. When she speaks, I hear her disdain, bright as a bell.

"How are we doing in here?"

We. She means me and the von Furstenberg. The von Furstenberg and I. She saw me out of the corner of her exquisitely lined eye going to the back of the store to retrieve it between the frigid Eileen Fishers and the smug Max Azrias and she disapproves. She knows the von Furstenberg is a separate entity, that it and I will never be one.

"Fine," I say. I remain absolutely still, try not to sound breathless. Like all is well. Just a regular shopping trip.

"Oh good," she says. "You let me know if you need anything." But in her voice I hear: *Give it up, fat girl.*

She knows I've been coveting the von Furstenberg ever since I first stood on the other side of her shop window, watching her slip it over a white, nippleless mannequin, looping some ropes of fake pearls around its headless neck. I didn't know it was a von Furstenberg then. I only knew it was precisely the sort of dress I dreamed of wearing when I used to eat muffins in the dark and watch Audrey Hepburn movies. Before I knew brands, I'd make lists of the perfect dresses—and when I saw this dress it was like someone, perhaps even God, had found the list and spun it into existence. Cobalt, formfitting, with a V in the front and one in the back. Cute little bows all down the butt crack, like your ass is a present. The sort of dress I'd wish to wear to attend the funeral of my former self, to scatter the ashes of who I was over a cliff's edge.

"Can I try this on?" I asked her.

Her eyes opened a little wider. Small glimmers of incredulity like slicks of oil.

"What? The von Furstenberg?"

"Yes."

She looked from the von Furstenberg to me, then back to the von Furstenberg, sizing both of us up. We two? Never we two.

Sighing, she led me to a fitting room, rearranging items as she went—insect hair clips, Baggallinis, peacock scarves—so it wasn't a totally wasted trip.

The whole time I was in there being asphyxiated by the von Furstenberg, I felt the fact of her clicking on the other side of the door, waiting for me to admit defeat, to come to my senses. Come on.

Today, though, I'm determined to prove her wrong. Today, I won't come out of the fitting room, let her snatch the mangled von Furstenberg from me, ask me, How did we do? as if she did not know how we did. As if she didn't already have the steamer turned on and ready to smooth out the creases of my failed struggle, a task she always undertakes with overdone tenderness. Then after I've left the store, through the shop window, I'll watch her pointedly press a damp rag all over the von Furstenberg, presumably to get rid of the slashes of Secret I leave behind. But those stains are always there when I come back. That's how I know it's all for show. Like, Look what you do, fat girl. Can't you take no for an answer? The von Furstenberg doesn't want you.

Well maybe I don't want the von Furstenberg. Has she ever thought of that? That maybe I despise it? That maybe I'm trapped in this dance with the von Furstenberg against my will?

Knock knock.

"Still all right in there?"

"Great," I say, and I'm tugging so hard on the back zipper, my tongue is lolling out of my mouth like I'm dead in a cartoon. But I feel it going up. Higher than it ever has before. And it's not a mirage, it fits. It's on. It's miraculous. And even though I'm panting, my hair in disarray from the struggle, I see we look immortal.

I'm just thinking how I'll wear it out of the store. Picturing how I'll pull back the curtain in the von Furstenberg, turn my zippered, von Furstenberged back to her and say, all casual, over my shoulder, Cut the tag, please? Maybe I'll even ask for a bag for my old dress—would she mind terribly putting my old dress in a bag? Mm? And that's when I see the jagged rip down the side seam. Maybe I couldn't hear the ripping over the sound of my own grunts. That happened once before, with the flesh-colored Tara Jarmon. It was impossibly tight when I bought it and then I was out one day walking, insisting, and it suddenly wasn't. It suddenly felt easy breezy, beautifully loose. I didn't understand. Until I caught a glimpse of myself in the reflective glass of an office building and saw the slashes on either hip.

Knock knock.

"We sure we're still doing okay in there?" Her voice says, A rat who insists on hitting its head again and again against the maze wall gets taken out of the maze. It gets escorted out, politely but firmly, by mall security.

"Yeah," I say, my hands fiddling with the zipper in a panic. But they're so slippery from all the exertion, I have to wipe them on the von Furstenberg just to get a grip. And the zipper still won't go down. I Gazelle. Five miles every morning with a photo of me in a no-name shroud taped to the little window that counts you down. Five miles, only to be told by the von Furstenberg in no uncertain terms that it counts for nothing.

"Do you need another size?" she asks. By "another" she of course means larger, which we both know isn't in stock.

I asked her once for a larger size and she said, *Let me check.* And then I loved her. Very briefly I loved her. Loved her hands clasped over her tweed-clad crotch. Loved the thin curl of her lips, a smirking red line. Loved all the bones in her ostrich throat, the arrowheads of her décolletage, her ash blond hair gathered in a glittery comb shaped like a praying mantis. Then, as she picked up the receiver, presumably to place the order, she said in a low voice, That will be five hundred dollars, please.

And I said, What?!

And she said, Well. Obviously you'll have to pay for it in advance. Or you could order it online on our website?

And I said, But I don't even know if it'll f—

And that's when I saw it, the smile on her face. The flicker of triumph. Like, Ha! You know and I know even the next size up wouldn't fit you, fat girl.

"I'm fine," I tell her now through my teeth, tugging with all my might.

I don't know how long I've been sitting here, half in and half out of the von Furstenberg, the pull tab of the zipper in the damp cave of my fist. My old dress, the one I thought I'd never have to wear again, lies like a jilted lover in the corner. I hear her clicking not too far off, rearranging the perfectly arranged merchandise—sequined hair clips shaped like butterflies, purses shaped like swans, perfumes that smell like very specific desserts and rains. I could just put my old dress over it. Go to the cash register. Explain. Offer to pay for the von Furstenberg. But the truth, as she well knows, is that even if it did fit, I cannot afford the von Furstenberg.

I have this terrible image of her coming in here with the jaws of life tucked under her arm. Ash blond tendrils escaping from her chignon as she attempts to wrench me out of the von Furstenberg. How the give of my flesh will be abhorrent to her hands, but not half as abhorrent as her bone white hands will be to my flesh. Other customers will look on as they pass by the open door like I'm a car crash in the opposite lane.

Or.

Or maybe I could learn to live like this.

As I sit here, I can already feel myself oozing out of the von Furstenberg. Oozing from the V in front and the V in the back, the volume of my ass threatening to crack the little bows along the fault line. And I begin to think maybe this is it. Maybe this is the only way out. Maybe, if I wait long enough, if I'm patient, I'll just ooze out. First the fat, then maybe we'll find a way to coax out the organs. Some organs I won't even need, like my appendix. Of course, even if we leave some things like my appendix behind, it'll be a slow process. Slow in terms of biological time, but not if you think say, geologically, like, in ages.

I'm patient.

Caribbean Therapy

It's my guilty pleasure, seeing Cammie over at Aria Lifestyle Salon during lunch hour for the Caribbean Hand Treatment. The salon's out of my way, south of the city center, and I can't really afford the treatment on my temp salary. Also, I don't know why but after Cammie's done with me, the skin around my nails peels and bleeds for days. Then there's the shoddy polish job that I further destroy, sometimes within minutes of walking out of there. Still. Every week, like clockwork, I'm compelled to call behind a closed door, like I'm calling for a sex worker.

"Hi," I whisper. I try to make the whisper easy breezy. "I'd like to make an appointment with Cammie."

"Cassie," the receptionist corrects.

"Cassie, right. I'd like to make an appointment with Cassie."

"What service?" Is there accusation in her voice? I can't tell.

When I tell the receptionist it's for the Caribbean Hand Treatment, there's silence, then a lot of typing. Too much typing. Heat creeps up the back of my neck. I grow nervous when she puts me on hold, when I'm forced to listen to the sound of Zen-like chimes encouraging patience. I am not patient. I begin to chew on my nails, which still bear traces of Bastille My Heart, from my last tryst with Cassie.

When at last she comes back on the line, she tells me there's a time issue. The thing is I like to schedule the Caribbean during lunch hour. I request noon in a tone that implies I have the full and important schedule of an executive and I'm squeezing it in between meetings, like it's my moment of Zen on a busy day in the financial or some such district. I'm told this is a busy time for Cassie. I'm reminded that Hattie, the other esthetician, is usually pretty open at this hour. Do I want Hattie? I remember Hattie, a pointy-faced young woman with bangs like Frankenstein's creature who looks like she's composed entirely of tendons, whose chest, under her smock, is almost completely concave. I tell them, No, I don't want Hattie, I want *Cammie*—Cassie, right.

Hunger yawns in me as I enter the salon on the appointed day. I am on nothing but oats and anger consumed over the sink at six a.m. But this is good, I think. I will not have lunch today. I will have Cammie. Cassie. Where is she? Panic seizes me, briefly, by the throat when I do not see her among the billowy-bloused, asymmetrically haired spa workers. Then I remember it's early. I am seventeen minutes early by my watch.

I tell myself I'm early not because I'm eager to see her but in order to enjoy the spa's many amenities. I sit in the waiting area and contemplate the crystalized ginger in its bowl. The toasted almonds and dried apricots in their respective glass jars. I watch other female clients partake of it all with tiny wooden tongs. Many of these women are in mid-treatment, some with their heads covered in tinfoil, from which tufts of colorless hair sprout. They leaf through magazines like *Shape* and *Prevention*, sipping complimentary licorice root–sweetened tea from handleless, dirt-colored cups. I flip through *Self* without really seeing, and feel as if I'm drowning—What if Cassie has forgotten me? What if she couldn't make it in today?—until I hear my name called like a question and I look up and there she is. Spilling out of a zebra-print maxi dress. Grinning crookedly at me between red corkscrew curls. My eye runs worriedly over her frame for any signs of weight loss. Seeing there are none, I breathe out. That Cassie is even fatter than I remember sates me in ways I cannot explain.

"Hi!" she says. "Elizabeth?"

"Liz."

"Liz, right. Follow me. They've got us all set up!"

I follow her broad back as she waddles over to the nail station.

"So what are we doing today?" she asks me. "Chocoholic? The Crème Brûlée?"

"The Caribbean."

"Ooh. That's my favorite."

At the station, the implements of the treatment lie at the ready: the edible ingredients in receptacles made to resemble cleaved coconut shells; the pointy silver instruments that she will employ clumsily, causing the aforementioned peeling and bleeding of my cuticle area; the stone bowl of hot salt water in which she will soak my hands—long and thin like Bela Lugosi's—one by one; Cassie herself, her bra straps digging into her shoulder flesh. An Olga? Freya, maybe? One of those brands with a Nordic-sounding name, which thank God I don't have to wear anymore. I can tell just by looking that Cassie bought hers too small.

"So is there an occasion we're getting ready for or . . . ?" Cassie asks me, leaving the question hanging.

Cassie likes there to be an occasion. There never is, but I pick one out of the air anyway.

"Museum opening," I say.

"Museum opening! That's exciting."

She seats herself across from me, making the stool underneath her creak. Nothing between us now but the narrow little station table. Underneath it, our kneecaps touch. And then comes the moment I pay the sixty-odd dollars for, the moment when she reaches across the table and slips my wedding ring off and takes my hands.

As usual, I apologize for how cold they are.

"Actually, it feels sort of nice." Cassie says. She always says something like that. A friend told me once that a stripper will tell every man she gives a lap dance to that he smells really good and what cologne is he wearing anyway? And she won't just say it. She'll breathe him in like his rank skin fumes are mountain air, like her lungs, let alone her little bunny slope nose, can't get enough.

"It's always so hot in here," Cassie says, blowing a lock of red hair off her face as if to prove it. Cassie's hands always feel warm and swollen, like they've been injected with some sort of hot gel. With her fingers, she traces my cracked nail beds, my peeling cuticles, the red, rough skin.

As usual, my hands make Cassie frown. But it's a tender frown, her sincere concern causing a small furrow to appear between her fawn-colored brows. She is concerned, rightly, that despite many Caribbean Therapy sessions, my hands are still in hideous shape. Am I not using that cuticle oil she gave me a sample of last time? I

am not, but I don't tell her this. I pretend like I'm confused. Like I
don't know what's going on either.

"Could it be the winter, maybe?" I offer. "It was pretty dry."

She says it could be—it *was* a dry one. She brings my hands
closer to her face. But it's more that they look picked at, she says.
Dry and cracked like I've been running them under hard, hot
water all day.

"Huh," I say. "Weird."

"Well, don't worry," she smiles. "We'll get you into shape."

"Thanks," I say, and she squeezes my hands a little, running her thumb pads over my index knuckles, causing me to sort
of sink into my seat.

We're still holding hands over the table. And it's always
awkward, that moment when she lets go, lowers one wrist into
the coconut shell of too-hot salt water.

"Temperature okay?"

"Great."

"So," she says, "Amuse Bouche? Hearts and Tarts?"

I pretend to weigh the options but honestly, these are Cassie's colors. I can't stand either of them. On my hands, so humor-
less, they look laughably pink. But I know Cassie hates the blood
and earth tones to which I'm naturally partial.

"How about Amuse Bouche? We'll do Hearts and Tarts
next time."

"I do love that one," she says.

"Me too."

She picks up a bottle of hot pink polish and shakes it, causing
her copious, freckled cleavage to ripple. I try not to look since
looking lights little parts of me on fire. Instead, I keep my gaze
focused on how her upper arm flesh bleeds out of her cap sleeves.

Not attractive, I tell myself, even though her flesh is young and firm. It won't always be firm, though. It'll grow old, I tell myself, just like Cassie. Whenever I'm hungry, which is often, I picture Cassie old. Her bloated body beneath a hospital bedsheet.

While she starts buffing and filing, we talk about what we've both been baking recently, even though I've baked nothing recently. But Cassie has always been baking something. Usually some white trash cake with a whorish-sounding name. Today, she tells me about one she made recently called Better Than Sex. "So yummy," she says.

"Sounds yummy," I say. When I'm around Cassie, I start using words like *yummy*, even though such words feel misshapen on my lips. I ask her how you make it, knowing I'll never make it, and she says, "Oh, easy peasy. First, you make devil's food cake. Like, from a box? Then you take a fork and just stab the hot cake all over. Then you pour caramel sauce and a thingy of condensed milk into the stab holes so the cake soaks it all up? Then you put it in the fridge for, like, three hours. Oh! And once it's chilled? You put whipped cream on top of *that*. So yummy."

"I'll have to try it." I'll never try it. "I did try your slutty brownies," I add.

"You did?!"

I didn't, of course. But I tell her all about how I brought them to work and how everyone loved them and begged for the recipe. So I gave it to them. I really hope that's okay with her.

"Of course!"

She applies the brown sugar exfoliant to my forearms, which will be followed by a yogurt moisture massage. The brown sugar chafes, the yogurt cools. It's an exhilarating combination. I close my eyes.

"So what have you been up to in the kitchen?" she asks me.

I think about the boneless skinless chicken breast I pounded into a thin white strip with a tenderizer last night, adding a squeeze of lime when I took it out of the oven to make it tropical tasting.

"Oh, just experimenting, mostly. Though I did make this bourbon bundt cake that turned out pretty good."

That wasn't me but my sadist coworker Eve. I bake and give everything away, Eve tells everyone, like it's a baking tip she's offering, like how you should add salt to chocolate. Eve always comes to work bearing a tin of some thickly iced treat, her wrist tendons visibly straining under the weight of her confection. She'll leave whatever she's made in the back room for all the fat and middling women we work with to cut thick slices out of.

"Oh, Eve, so delicious!"

"Oh, good!" Eve beams. When Eve beams, the corners of her mouth turn downward, her eyes crinkle almost closed, and the hollow in her throat gets disconcertingly deeper.

By the end of the shift, the tin's more or less empty except for crumbs. And Eve's over the sink, rinsing it with steaming hot water, smug. Often, she forgets to rinse the tin and I have to do it. Even though I've told her time and time again she can't leave leftovers on the counter like that overnight. Because of ants.

We're on to the elbow-to-fingertip yogurt massage. When Cassie kneads my bony palm like it's a ball of dough, grabbing hold of each long finger and pulling it gently between her plump ones, I never know where to look. She never knows where to look either. What we both end up doing is looking at the space just past our respective left ears.

"A bourbon bundt," Cassie repeats, calling me back. And I

watch her try to picture it with the hungry eye of her mind. "Sounds yum. I'll have to make it for my husband. He loves that Southern rustic stuff."

Cassie got married recently. I couldn't believe it when she first told me. At first, I thought it might have to do with the fact that she's part of a very small religious community, people who see each other with the eyes of Jesus first. Then I found out Cassie isn't really part of this community anymore, at least not hard-core, and that the guy just happened to be a friend of her brother's who thought she was cute. And the thing is *he's* cute. At least according to the picture Cassie showed me once on her iPhone.

She shows me another picture of him now.

I take the phone and stare at the picture like it's a pot of water I'm trying to boil, waiting for any latent sign of his freakdom to surface. A yellowish tinge to the skin, maybe? Some pervert shading under the eyes? A weird nose kink, but no. As far as I can see, he's the stuff of the earth. Its handsome salt. I'm still looking when at last she takes the phone from my hands and says, "He's pretty cute, huh?"

"He is. How did—well, congratulations."

I ask if they're still in their honeymoon period and she blushes. Yes, yes they are. It's sort of wonderful.

"That's great," I say. "Really, great." It is.

"It is," she says. She's very lucky. "How are things with your husband?"

I look at her, eyes wide at her innocent question, and that's when a video clip of two fat girls in ill-fitting bondage gear flogging one another on the floor of a fake-looking dungeon, the one I found in my husband's recent web history last year, comes back to me in full graphic detail. I found others that night: fat girls dressed as French maids, Ukrainian lesbians, hopeful cheerleaders. Fat girls who always seem to be smirking or looking surprised that their clothes are too tight. Fat girls who, along with a few sites about trance music and conspiracy theories, had been worming their way into his web history for several months.

I say things are great, and feel the corner of my mouth do one of those spastic quivers.

"That's so great," she says. "How long have you guys been married again?"

"Going on three years in July."

"Ooh, so big anniversary coming up."

"Yeah."

"We could do a shimmery color for that. Maybe something peach."

By then she's painting Amuse Bouche on my fingernails and she's all hunched over me, frowning in her effort to be precise. But she isn't precise. She makes all these mistakes, which she has to keep fixing with a sharp little wooden stick she keeps dipping into acetone. It's at this moment that I want to wrench my fingers back from her hot hands. For I cannot bear the weight of her any longer. Her warm, fat touch becomes the opposite of comfort, it becomes oppressive. I need to be free of her. Now.

"We done?" I ask her. Underneath the table, I'm tapping my foot.

"Just need to do the topcoat," she smiles.

When at last she's administered the quick-drying serum from the eyedropper, she says, "Now just sit tight for a bit while it dries."

But I can't bear to be at that table any longer. Once she's moved her fleshy knees and taken the bowl away in which I soaked my hands, it's as if I'm at a wake. As she dumps the salty water into the sink, she asks me, as always, if I'd like to keep the emery board. At first I thought this was a tender gesture, a thing between Cassie and me. I found out later that they all ask this question. Still, I always keep the emery board. In my bathroom, there's a whole drawer full of these emery boards beneath the sink.

Not too long ago, my husband opened the drawer and said, What the hell is this? And I said, Emery boards. Emery boards, huh, he said. Whatever. And he shut the drawer with a shrug.

When at last we're finished, Cassie slides my ring back on, carries my purse up to the register so as not to compromise my Amuse Bouched nails. She fishes for my wallet. Roots around through my endless packets of Have Your Dessert and Chew It Too! gum for my car keys. I've got every flavor in there from Apple Pie to Sweet Tropical.

I say sorry it's such a swamp in there. And she says don't apologize, I should see *her* purse. She reminds me my nails are still quite tacky, so be careful. This is a slow-drying, formaldehyde-free topcoat. Sure, that top layer will feel dry-*ish* in about fifteen minutes, but those layers underneath will take a while. So don't go banging them up against a wall or anything, hahaha.

Hahaha, I agree. And I promise Cassie I'll be careful, knowing already I won't be.

After I leave Aria, I do try to drive carefully, only lightly gripping the steering wheel. Every time there's a red light, I look down at my nails, the color of Barbie innards, winking in the light. Already there's a slight dent on one nail, a slight wrinkling of the topcoat on a couple of others.

By the time I get back to the shop, I'll have more or less massacred them.

When I walk through the shop doors, I see Eve there behind the cash desk, draped in her usual iridescent silks. Seeing me come in, she beams like she's a drowning woman and I'm a buoy being tossed to her from a ship. My arrival means she can finally go out into the back alley and scarf her unripe peach, her tub of fat-free Greek yogurt sprinkled sparingly with some sort of seedling. If she's really famished, she might peck at a handful of almonds, which she'll count out first in her palm like pills. They come from a Costco container, onto which she has scrawled "Do Not Eat! Eve's ☺" with a Sharpie. Unbeknownst to Eve, I steal from this container all the time.

I smile at her as I come in, but I pretend I don't see her look of hungry desperation and go straight to the back room. There, I take my time reapplying my cupcake lip gloss in the cracked mirror, even though it really needs no reapplication. But after seeing Cassie, I like to briefly inspect my own facial hollows and angles. It's a relief to see they're all still there. That I didn't get fat by proxy. There's a bundt cake on the counter, obviously Eve's handiwork. Banana with some sort of obscure berry in it—maybe lingon or goose. Already it's been more or less eaten. I picture all my middling colleagues coming in one by one to cut themselves a slice with our dull communal knife. Patricia, who's been on the seventeen-day diet for the past five years. Mary, Sarah, and Lynne, all of whom are on some sort of point system. Madeline, who is attempting common sense to no avail. When I open the collective mini-fridge, I find their containers of wilted Organic Girl, their expired fat-free vinaigrettes, and, of course, Eve's stalwart tub, atop which sits her white-fleshed peach, like a crown you want to topple.

There's some Soy Delicious! and a Fuji in there for me too, for later. For now, I grab a handful of Eve's almonds. I chew them, my eyes on her half-eaten bundt. I can tell by the flourish of grooves on the cake's surface that she used the tiered blossom mold today. She likes to use a fun mold. Funky, she'd say, though the word rings wrong in her mouth. I picture her in her prim kitchen, pulling it out of the oven with festive pot holders, gloating. The treadmill she walks on every day just down the dark hall. Also gloating. At first I try to be above it, but then I grab the blunt knife dripping in the sink.

I've just stuffed a thin slice in my mouth when the swinging doors creak open and there's Eve. Still beaming, but her eyes say I've kept her waiting long enough. She's taking matters into her own hands.

"Amber's covering the desk for me," she says. "I'm *famished*."

I nod, trying not to show her that I'm chewing, but she's seen, so I have to say, "Delicious."

Eve opens her silvery eyes wide, feigning innocence.

"Your bundt."

"Oh, good!"

"Sorry I'm late," I say, swallowing. "Lunch took a while."

"No worries, kiddo," she says, giving my shoulder a little squeeze. Then she leans in, sniffs. "Mm, you smell good enough to eat." She looks at my banged-up nails. "Amuse Bouche?"

"Hearts and Tarts," I say, curling my fingers into my palms and hiding them from her view.

She looks at me. "Sharp."

With my mouth still full of Eve's bundt, I take up her place at the cashier's desk. Watch her pass by me as she makes her way toward the alley, clutching her lunch and a photography book of Paris to her sternum. She'll thumb through the pictures while she eats her yogurt. Her lunch ritual.

Behind the desk, I sit staring at our sideline merchandise, which Eve has arranged in complex, precarious towers by the cash register. Whimsical things you never thought you needed until you found yourself standing in line in front of them. Women clad in gym wear they never seem to change out of come in saying, *How cute! How cute!* Reminding me of the birdcalls I hear whenever I pass the aviary on my twice-daily walk.

I look at Amber sitting beside me at the desk, eating a muffuletta from the deli next door, smirking at Facebook on her phone.

I inspect my nails. Apart from a little more topcoat wrinkling, they've held together. I look at the jar of saltwater taffy Eve always keeps by the cash register, then at my watch.

"Eve's taking a while," I say to Amber.

She shrugs, keeps smirking at her screen, chewing. "Not like we're busy or anything."

"Still."

I get up and wander over to a picture hanging just to the left of the back door, some sort of abstract landscape that looks vaguely vaginal. Through the glass in the door, I see Eve out there in the alley, sunning herself on a cracked plastic chair, *Paris in Color* splayed open on her iridescent lap to the photo of the Luxembourg gardens. The peach pit and yogurt tub sit ravished at her callused heels. She's clutching a mug of green tea I know she takes unsweetened. Staring straight ahead, past the dumpsters, into some Zen space, I imagine. Perhaps an ocean. Rolling gray waves. A stony beach. Eve's recently divorced. Lives with her dogs in an empty house on a hill with a view of the desert. Terrible to love the water as much as I do and live in a desert, she confided to me once. There's the lake, I told her. Lake shmake, Eve said. What my soul needs is the sea. With my eyes on her now, I adjust the picture frame, scraping the wall with my nails a little as I do. Eve starts in her chair at the noise and snaps her head to look at me through the glass door. I smile at her and turn away.

At home, he's in his office with the door closed. When I open it, I expect I don't know what. But what I find is only lines of code and him innocently clicking.

He turns to look at me. "Hey."

"Dinner?" I ask from the doorframe.

"I got Barbacoa on the way home," he says, holding up a large bit-into burrito. Waving it like a flag of peace. Two tiny wedges of squeezed lime sit on his desk beside a dripping Coke.

"Figured you'd want to do your own thing," he says. "You know. For your diet."

"Oh, okay. I guess I'll just make myself a salad, then."

"Okay."

I turn to go, then stop.

"What?" he says.

"Would you like to at least eat with me?" I ask him. "When I've made it?"

"Well, by then this'll be cold so, you know, I should probably eat now. But I could sit with you, if you'd like."

I picture him sitting in front of me, hands clasped on the table. Him watching me chew, then swallow, then chew.

"No, it's okay, you've got work." I close the door.

I eat a bowl of lightly dressed spring mix while leafing through *Nigella Bites*, which I thought for sure would have a Better Than Sex Cake recipe. It doesn't. So I watch the YouTube clip of her making a caramel croissant bread pudding after a late night out. A bit eccentric for supper, she confesses to the camera, stepping out of her heels, dropping her earrings onto the kitchen counter. Nonetheless, it's what I need. Smilingly swirls sugar in the saucepan. High heat—don't be timid. Now, you can swirl as the caramel heats up but NEVER stir. If you stir, you can make the sugar crystalize and what I want, what anyone wants, is a luscious, smooth—

The door to his office opens. He comes out to throw away his Barbacoa bag, looking askance at me and Nigella.

"I sent you a link to a new Nick Cave song earlier today. Did you listen to it?"

"Not yet."

"You should check it out," he says. He goes back to the office, shutting the door.

Eggs, milk, and—why not?—cream. Stale croissants, which are not really good for anything except this. Where they are sublime. Ooh. I can feel the butter of the croissants on my fingers—that's what's going to make this so delicious. Fit for angels to eat on their clouds, though obviously they'd have to be very weight-bearing clouds, hahaha. Slips it into the oven. Here you go, my darling.

I watch the clip again, while chewing five sticks of Have Your Dessert and Chew It Too! gum at the same time. Apple Pie, Mint Chocolate Chip Ice Cream, and Orange Crème Pop all at once. Mmm, Nigella says, pulling the pan out of the oven. At this point, she's changed into a black silk kimono patterned with dragons. Dessert for dinner, she murmurs, dishing herself a bowlful to take into the bedroom. Everyone's dream.

I watch it again and again, chewing until my eyes water and my vision gets blurry around the edges and a disconcerting throbbing begins above my left ear. I pick at my nails.

"You're back soon," Cassie says, taking my hands. The heat of them makes me feel slightly drunk on contact.

"I'm such a klutz," I say, shaking my head. And I tell her how, believe it or not, I did end up banging my nails against a wall, hahaha. She hahahas along with me but she's regarding me curiously, so I add, "Also, I have an event tonight."

"Ooh, what's the event?" Her blue eyes go very bright.

"Dinner?" But this doesn't seem like enough. "And a musical."

Her eyes say I'm going to have to tell her which musical.

"Phantom?"

"I *love* Phantom!" In fact, her husband took her to see it recently for her birthday. They made a whole night out of it—so fun oh my god. Well, she says, taking my hands more tightly in hers, we definitely have to get me into shape for that!

She runs her fingers over my cuticles and nail beds, debating whether she should use a buffer. I resist the urge to close my eyes.

"Tired?" she asks me.

"A little. Having a hard time sleeping lately."

"Oh," she looks up at me, the furrow deepening between her brows. "I'm sorry. Well, go ahead and close your eyes if you want to," she smiles. "I won't judge. Better here than at Phantom, right?"

"Right."

She's wearing a turquoise peasant blouse today that brings out her eyes, the peach in her skin. I see she's gotten some sun since I saw her last. Her red curls are brushed up off her neck in one of those careless buns I can never pull off.

While she files, I say that it sounds like her husband really went all out for her birthday.

"Oh yeah, I got seriously spoiled the whole day. So fun."

"Tell me."

She tells me how he made her pancakes in the morning. Then he took her to the zoo, which was super fun. There's a new polar bear exhibit—have I seen it? Oh my gosh, I *have* to. Then, oh! They went for cupcakes at Sweet Diva, that new cupcake place that just opened? She picks up the buffer, then puts it down. "I won't buff these just 'cause we did them so recently? We don't want your nail beds to get too thin on top of everything else." She pats my hands, then drops them back into the salt water bowls.

"I've never been to Sweet Diva," I tell Cassie.

"Oh! You should go. With all the baking you do, you'd so appreciate it," she says. "They do this coconut cream that's out of this world. Probably we had too many. Had to have a nap after."

As she covers my arms with cold yogurt, I picture her and her non-freak husband napping. On a quilted bedspread. Cassie making a deep dent in the mattress. Maybe he's got his arm around her.

"Then after the nap?" I prompt.

She smiles. "He gave me my presents."

"What'd he get you?"

"This nail art kit I wanted," she says, flashing her freshly coiffed nails at me. Each nail is embossed with a badly painted flower.

"Pretty."

"Also these," she says, wiggling her feet at me from under the table. I look down and see that her feet are encased in cheap, vaguely oriental-looking sandals stuccoed with small bits of brightly colored plastic. I see her husband kneeling before her, smilingly slipping them onto her small feet. She has disconcertingly tiny feet.

"Nice."

We're on to the massage portion. I close my eyes for a while.

"Where did he take you to dinner?"

"Oh, just this Italian place in the mall I really like. You know the one with the pretty waterfall?"

Cassie and her husband seated across from each other at a dinner table. He's wearing a smart tie, beaming at her beaming at him over quivering candlelight. He takes her coiffed hand and kisses it. Maybe they're talking about their favorite zoo animals.

"Oh, right. I love that place." I hate that place. "What did you have?"

"This creamy pasta dish? With the little bowtie pasta. What are those called again?"

They're in the half-dark of their bedroom, on their nap-rumpled bed. Would she want the lights off? Probably lowered. He'd have to be on top. Maybe not.

"Farfalle," I say.

"Farfalle," she repeats. "That's it! And then this chocolate lava cake for dessert. So yummy."

She straddles him under her white skirt, blouse sliding off her shoulders. For a brief moment I inhabit his shuddery skin. Lying on my back on the Cassie-dented mattress, between her broad thighs. Feeling her opening my shirt button by button, my tie being tugged by her primped hands. When she leans in to kiss me, a coil of red hair grazes my cheek and her sleeves slide farther down her shoulders and I feel the full weight of Cassie. She tastes of flavored balm and lava cake and hot day. A tinfoil swan of leftover lava cake sits on the dresser, watching.

I open my eyes.

"Where did you go there?" she laughs.

"Nowhere. Sounds like a perfect day."

"It was," she says, beaming at the nothing just past my left ear. Unlike Eve, her beam creates no hollows.

"So what's the occasion?" my husband says, looking worriedly at the waterfall, at the faux frescoes on the ceiling designed to emulate Tuscany.

"I just thought it would be nice to have dinner out together for once." I try beaming.

He shrugs and cracks open the oversize menu. Then he closes it again.

"I'm surprised you picked this place," he says, staring at the vast basket of oily breadsticks between us. They're sprinkled with a yellow saltlike substance designed to resemble cheese.

"I thought it would be fun," I say.

He raises an eyebrow, then shakes his head and opens the menu again.

"What?"

"Nothing."

"I'm going to have the farfalle," I announce.

"Okay," from behind his menu.

"And after I thought maybe we could get some cupcakes. At Sweet Diva, that new place that just opened? They supposedly do a great coconut cream." I try beaming some more but he just looks at me.

"*What?*" I ask him.

"Nothing." He looks back into the menu. "I just don't want it to go dark is all."

"Dark? I don't know what you mean *dark*. It's just dinner."

He lowers the menu and sighs.

"You know how you are. I wish it could just be dinner too. But whenever we go out like this it's never just dinner, it's this downward spiral, this kamikaze of guilt."

Tears fill my eyes, but I suck them back. I nod at the bread basket.

"I'm sorry. I'm being an ass." He takes my hands, but the grip is lax. Noticing the nail polish, he says, "Nice."

"I just got them done today."

"Didn't you *just* get your nails done, like, a few days ago?"

"Yeah."

He lets go of my hands.

"What's wrong?"

"I just want you to be happy is all."

"I know. I am."

"Good," he says. "Me too."

"You are?"

"Of course. Why?"

I think again about the night when I watched that video of the two fat maids on his desktop. Felt his office door opening behind me. Saw his worried reflection in the window above the screen. Heard him call my name like a question from the doorframe, call with impossible softness, a softness I hadn't heard in so long, like his voice was fingers, stroking the face of my name. I didn't answer or turn around, I just kept watching, my hands curled into fists.

"No reason," I say now.

"You've been so distant since your mother died. Honestly, Elizabeth, I haven't known how to handle it. I don't know what to do."

Liz, I think. I told you I go by Liz now. Why can he never get it right?

"This has nothing to do with my mother," I lie. "At all. I'm fine."

And I sit there, watching him chomp breadsticks and regard the waterfall sullenly, thinking how there was a time, not too long ago, when with my formerly swollen hands, I could have snapped him in two. A time when I was afraid to lean against him if we were watching TV on the couch because I worried the weight of me was too much. That if I rolled over at night, I'd accidentally crush him to death. It was a ridiculous fear—I was never that big—but it kept me up nights. That and my own hunger.

After we get home from dinner that night, I go to the couch and he goes to his office, shutting the door behind him. I lie awake on the couch, staring at the silhouette of my mother's urn on the mantel. I keep the pictures of her in an ornamental box marked *Paris*. In some of them we are both about Cassie's size. Then it's just my mother who is about Cassie's size, and she's looking at

my shrunken frame happily and I'm looking at the camera like I
have no idea. Like I'm vacant. And I can see her illness, the diabetes and heart disease she never wanted to discuss, in the sheen
on her skin, its flushed color, how her eyes are too bright, how
tired she looks, so very tired, I never realized how tired until
now. On the end table is a photo of Tom and me on her balcony,
from the afternoon when he met her for the first time. He's wearing a tie because this is the first time he's meeting my mother.
I'm wearing that dress I've never worn since. We're standing
side by side, but looking off in different directions—him at the
camera, me at something off in the corner. I'm in open-toed
heels, the toes freshly painted by my mother the night before.
She didn't just paint them, she clipped them, scrubbed the cal-
luses off my heels. We were sitting on the balcony, and I said I
wanted a pedicure and bitched that I couldn't afford one and she
said, *Jesus Christ,* and got up and left. I thought I had just pissed
her off by complaining. But a few minutes later, she returned,
panting a little, a towel over her broad shoulder, some old bottles
of polish in one hand and a well-worn pumice stone in the other.
She draped the towel over one thigh, then patted her thigh with
her palm. *Here,* she said. Leaning back in her cast iron chair, I
propped my foot on her thigh like it was an ottoman, and then
for several minutes, there was my mother's heavy frame bent
over me, clipping and scraping and painting in silence, concentrating so hard her tongue slid out between her lips, because she
really had no idea how to paint toenails, while I looked past her
at the sun setting behind her over the lake. It was awkward
because we never really touched, and yet here was all my mother's flesh hunched over one foot. We did a blood red, which

was the only color she had besides clear. It was one of the last times that she and I would be alone.

There, she said, slightly breathless, when she was done. *How's that?*

Good, thanks, I said, my eyes to the right of her, fixed on the lake, the sun setting over it, not able to take her in just then.

She's holding my hands up to the light to see if she should cut the cuticles. I'm staring at her breasts caged in flesh-colored lace. The sight makes my eyes sting. A tear, unbidden and hot, slides down my cheek. With the crook of an elbow, I brush it hastily away.

"You okay?" The furrow of concern deepens between her brows but today I am not moved, today I hate her for it.

"Fine."

"You sure?"

She's wearing a long, light blue sundress with thin, slippy straps. I remind myself of the store she had to buy it in. I look at how the straps sliding from her shoulders expose the thick bra straps beneath, which are a sad flesh tone. How heavy her burden, I tell myself. How hot she must feel in the sun. I even do the hospital visualization. But it's no good. All I see is how the blue shade of the dress matches her eyes and the bright sky in the windows behind her. How she's gotten even more of a tan over the past few days. Her red hair looks lighter, is grazing the sun-freckled flesh of her shoulder, now more brown than peach.

"Just tired," I tell her. "I haven't been sleeping much."

"Oh, right. I'm sorry."

"Me too."

She still has my hands in hers.

"I bet you sleep well, though," I say. "I bet most nights you're out like a light."

"Yeah," she says, dropping my hands into the salt water bowls. "I don't have too much trouble there."

"You're lucky. I've never been able to just drop off like that. Water's a bit hot."

"Sorry! I always try to get it on the hot side just 'cause it cools down so quickly? But I can—"

"It's all right. It'll cool down soon enough."

"Well"—scooping brown sugar into her palms—"hopefully this'll relax you a bit. Feel free to close your—"

"Cassie, are you happy?"

She looks up. Her brow's still furrowed, probably from concentrating.

"Am I happy?" She blinks.

"In your life. With your husband?"

She lowers her eyes so her lashes cuddle each cheek. They're so long and thick and perfectly curled, I asked her once if they were fakes. They aren't. I still don't believe it.

"Pretty much. I mean, for the most part yes. Why?"

"No reason."

We're silent for a bit.

She starts rubbing my forearm with what feels like a new force. I watch the sugar crystals dig into and chafe my skin.

"I mean," she adds, staring at my arm, "sure, we have *some* problems. Who doesn't?"

"Right. Of course."

I look at her and smile until her gaze goes sideways and lowers to my sugar-ravaged hands.

"Why?" she says. "Why are you asking?"

"No reason. Look, do you mind if we do another color today? Sort of had my fill of Amuse Bouche."

We go back to contemplating the space just past our respective left ears.

She continues to rub the brown sugar into my already raw arms with excruciating vigor, making her breast flesh ripple way more than it really needs to, I think. After she rinses it off roughly with a scalding hot cloth, she scoops cold white yogurt from the coconut shell. I watch her slather it onto my scaly forearm, work it between my slender fingers with her warm, plump hands. Even when my hands were plump like Cassie's, they never gave off such warmth.

"I just don't get it," I say.

"What don't you get?" There's a new coolness in her voice. The shock of it makes my heart skip. For a second I'm speechless.

I look at the red coil of hair that has slipped from her messy bun onto her broad freckled shoulder, her thin sky blue strap and the thick flesh-colored bra strap beneath. I feel the tightness of my own dress buttons down my back.

"What don't you get?" she prompts.

"Why they call this the Caribbean. Because there's nothing really 'Caribbean' about it, is there? I mean, ingredient-wise?" It's true. The yogurt's not even Greek.

Cassie says nothing.

"Must make you hungry, though, this combination," I say. "Does it?"

She looks at me until I lower my eyes.

"At first it did," she says. "Yeah. Although," she adds, "rubbing it on people's hands and feet enough times can make you pretty sick of it after a while."

She puts the polish and topcoat on quickly. She's sloppy administering the serum from the eyedropper, so the clear liquid bleeds out of my nail beds in rivulets. She doesn't enlist me to stay and wait those ten minutes that she always says would make all the difference in the world. She just takes the bowl and dumps the cooled salt water into the sink.

"You want this?" She asks as an afterthought, dangling the emery board over the trash bin, holding it between her thumb and index finger like it's the tail of roadkill.

"I'm good."

She doesn't carry my purse to the register, so that I pretty much destroy my nails fishing out my keys and wallet. But I still leave her an absurd cash tip. I write "For Cammie" on the little gratuity envelope. Then I cross it out and write "Cassie."

These days I wake to the smell of whatever she's been baking since before dawn—that is, if I'm really sleeping. Seven-layer coconut cakes. Lattice-crust pies full of cherries she hand pits. Often I'll have a slice or two while she watches from the other end of the dining room table. Just until I find my own place, I tell Eve each morning when I join her in the kitchen. Stay as long as you like, she says, watching me fork into her dessert, pouring us both more coffee. Not like I don't have the room.

This morning, I rise from her plastic-covered couch and look at her view of the desert through her compulsively Windexed windows. I see a lake made of salt. An already too-high sun that's blinding. A parched landscape, so far from the one I grew up in.

Come home, my father said in a voice mail. He'd tried calling me at the apartment and Tom had told him I'd left. *Just come back. Use your mother's money and put a down payment on a place out here. There's no reason for you to be out there anymore. Just come home.* I think of calling him back now. Instead I look up Mel's contact info on my cell phone, my finger hovering over the call button while I stare at her name. She and I haven't talked much at all since I moved out here, though I did call her a few weeks ago one night when I was first sleeping at Eve's. It was awkward. She was pretty miserable, she said, and when I asked why, she said she and her boyfriend were having problems, that she hated her job, and worst of all, she'd gained weight. She didn't want to talk about it. I said she was being too hard on herself, it happened to everyone, and anyway I was sure she was still beautiful. I meant it. When she said nothing, I told her I was feeling miserable too. I told her about me and Tom. It was hard because so much time had passed and there was so much she didn't know. I told it in fragments that felt insubstantial, that seemed to come apart as I spoke, that didn't appear to add up to anything at all against the scrutiny of her silence. Telling her made it all seem petty, somehow. When I finally trailed off, she said, *That sounds rough. I'm sorry.*

I think of Tom down there in the parched valley, behind his office door. Maybe he doesn't even know I'm gone. I think of Cassie and her husband, what adventures they might be up to today. Or perhaps it's a lazy day. They've drawn the curtains, are lolling about on their island of couch, he's kissing the thin white strip of shoulder under her straps that the sun never catches.

When I called Aria the other day, I was told Cassie was booked solid. I was offered Hattie. It was like that one time I went to For

Your Eyes Only and asked for the voluptuous redhead, and what they gave me instead was this thin Caribbean girl with poorly done streaks. These days I go to this Vietnamese place down the road Eve recommended. *It isn't so la-dee-dah,* she warned, *but they get the job done.* There are only two kinds of hand treatments— Basic and Spa—and the only difference is paraffin. There's no food in the waiting area either, just a fishbowl full of what looks like licorice but turned out to be nothing but slippery black stones. The one perk is that the proprietress hammers at your upper back and shoulders with her smooth little fists while you're waiting for your nails to dry. It's a nice touch, Eve says, and I agree. Also, she'll do whatever color you want without comment. She'll paint my nails the black-red I love, which will make them look dipped in vampire blood. And at the end of the treatment, when she offers me the emery board, I shake my head no every time. Because what the hell am I going to do with it anyway? She nods and chucks it in the bin, where it belongs. That's our ritual. I tip her exactly 15 percent.

Additionelle

Since I've returned home, I sometimes feel compelled to come back here. The sight of the plus-size mannequins in the shop window still soothes me. The outward undulation of stomach as comforting as an ocean wave. Their outfits look surprisingly current, almost hip. Skirts that nearly fishtail. Polka-dot bustiers. Things with eyelets and things edged with lace—and not weird plus-size lace either. Only when you look more closely, observe the generous cuts, the longer hemlines, three-quarter-length sleeves, do you see how they give themselves away as clothes for those with something to hide.

When I enter the shop, I see the familiar stepped display of boatneck T-shirts, the ones emblazoned with iron-on appliqués of various animals. Mainly varieties of cat. Cheetahs. Tigers. Domestic shorthairs gleefully swiping at balls of yarn. The animals regard me with those sequined eyes that, in former years, when I couldn't shop anywhere else, I used to dream of gouging out. The music they play in here hasn't changed. Instrumental variants of soul tunes still drip from unseen speakers. Songs with lyrics that always seem to revolve around the word *woman*. You make me feel like a natural woman. When a man loves a woman, etc. As if the idea of being a woman in here requires convincing. I watch the fat female shoppers within pawing through the racks, presumably hunting for The Least of All Evils: a black cardigan without rhinestone jetties or webs of pearl across the front; a stretchy unadorned V- or scoop neck. Back when I had to shop here, I used to do the same. I'd spend hours hunting for something—anything—that would render me moderately fuckable. And if not fuckable, something in which I could grieve over the fact of not being fuckable with unbaubled dignity. I make my way through these racks, among these women, not one of them anymore, and yet one of them still, and it's as though I've never left. I really should stop coming here.

The saleslady, seeing me hold up a zebra-patterned A-line dress, asks if she can help me. She doesn't recognize me, of course. How could she? It's been years since I've shopped here and I've lost God knows how much in that time, maybe a full-grown woman. Also, I went by a different name. Also, I never used to come in here alone, but with my mother.

Though my mother also had to shop here, make do with Addition Elle slacks and sweaters, she, like this saleswoman, always wore a necklace that matched her earrings that matched her bag that matched her shoes. She called this "jazzing it up." My mother and this saleswoman got along famously.

The saleswoman doesn't remember me, but I remember her. Her jewelry is still aggressively cheerful, still screams, I'm trying to make the best of things. But whereas once she spoke to me kindly via my mother, her tone with me now is suspicious, her eyes dipping down my body to size me up. I'm not within the 14-to-24 range. What the hell am I doing here?

Just looking, thanks, I tell her.

She glances sideways at her colleague, who is folding monster bras under a FUNCTIONAL CAN BE SEXY sign. I smile at them both warmly, like I'm spreading my arms open wide, like these are my sisters. They smile back doubtfully. What, am I mocking them?

I feel her following me as I weave my way through the boleros and heavy chain-mail dresses that make up Evening Wear, so I grab a couple of dresses off the rack at random. A striped caftan. Something gold and shoulder padded for old times' sake. I'm about to head for the fitting room when I spot a calf-length midnight blue velvet dress with puffed sleeves cinched with rhinestone buckles hanging on a rack close by. I pull it off the rack and replace the others, turn toward the saleswoman, who has indeed been trailing me this whole time.

She looks at me, uncertain. Do I want a fitting room? Really? I really do?

I nod. Yes. I do.

She leads me back with palpable reluctance.

The fitting room is exactly as I remember it.

All mirrors and merciful lighting. The door, thick and bolted, made of reinforced steel that goes right to the floor. No terrible smurf I can't see on the other side of this wall, squawking for a size 0 or an extra-extra small. Apart from the heavy rustle of thick thighs straining against slacks, everyone's silent. Through the wall, I hear a woman tell another woman that the pants look fine, no, no, they look just fine. Inside, there's a wide padded bench so you can see if something embarrassing happens when you sit down. The bench I used to sit on with folded arms in a monster bra the color of gunmetal. All the sweater sacks and stirrup pants I was supposed to be trying on lying at my feet like kicked cats. Shaking my head. Being difficult. My mother and the saleswoman knocking on the door. *Let's see!* Or sometimes my mother would come in with me and sit there, watch me change into and out of things. It looks fine, she'd say. She said that every time except once, when she turned away, attempting to mask her disgust at the sight of the fresh mess of red stretch marks across my stomach. Even though she had the same marks on her own stomach, she couldn't bear seeing them on me. Hadn't she tried, in her way, to spare me from inheriting her fate? I can still see them now in the mirror, faded.

I hang the dress on a hook on the back of the door, run my hands over the fuzzy velvet. Give or take a few details, this is more or less the dress. An updated version bearing the brunt of the latest trends. The same midnight blue shade my mother said was "black enough, Jesus," knowing no dress sold in this store was ever black enough for me. The same buckles, affixed lamely to the puffed sleeves, that I remember trying so hard to rip off. I even got Mel's aunt, who was a seamstress, to try to remove them legitimately. She stood there under my armpit for nearly a half hour, a frowning Slovenian elf, a cigarette dangling from her hairy lip, pulling and pulling on the buckle, then shaking her head like a doctor at a lost cause. *No,* she said at last, *I cannot remove without damaging sleeves.*

So do it anyway, I wanted to say. But all I said was, *Oh.*

Meanwhile Mel stood nearby like an innocent bystander, corseted in brocade and fishtailed in velvet, switching from a concerned expression to sneak pleased peeks at herself in the full-length mirror. In three hours from that moment, I knew I'd be watching her wrapped around some mangy Goth boy on the dance floor, her front laces undone, her skirt hitched up high, while I leaned against a nearby wall watching and counting the minutes to pizza on the sidewalk.

I take the dress off the hanger now, hold it up against me.

I ended up getting some action in it, if you can believe it. Fetish night at Savage Garden. A silver-shirted boy with sea urchin hair. Mel had dragged me there against my will, then spent the whole night making out with some man who resembled a melancholy pirate. I was wearing this velvet atrocity, feeling hideous, leaning against a wall, German industrial music deafening my ears, watching a half-naked woman affixed to a wooden cross get lashed repeatedly in the middle of the dance floor. And he came up to me. First he downed a pitcher of beer, then he wiped his mouth with the back of his hand, then he came up to me. I thought surely he'd go for the emaciated girl in the black halter to my left, but no, it was me he was walking toward, me he took outside and pushed against a brick wall, my face he cupped between his hands to the point where I nearly couldn't breathe. But what was most beautiful? Was how he put his hands up that terrible dress, ripping it on the side, it was so tight. *Oops,* he said, but I didn't mind, in fact, it gave me an idea. And when I asked him to he tore at the buckles. Tore them off both sides with one swift movement, while my hands clutched his hair. The sound of those rips. The *clink clink* sound of the rhinestones hitting the dirty, spit-strewn pavement was the single most erotic experience of my life, until Mel tore me out from under him.

It looked like he was assaulting you, she told me later on the streetcar home.

Well, he wasn't, I said.

Well, it looked like he was. She was irritated. The pirate had had to leave early. She'd been stuck watching me for once.

What the hell happened to you? my mother asked me when I came home.

Fell, I told her.

Knock knock from outside the fitting room. Her voice trying for easy breezy: "Are we okay in there?"

We. Why always *we?* What am I?

"We're fine, thanks," I tell her.

Later, years later, when I'd shrunk, I saw him standing on the corner of Queen and Spadina, waiting for a streetcar. No more blond spikes or metallic shirts. He had brown thinning hair now. Just a man waiting for a streetcar in tan corduroy. I was in my car, waiting for the light to change. There was no way I could've got out then, but it felt like I had to say something. But then the light changed, and even though I searched for him in my rearview mirror I didn't see him.

The saleslady's voice is shrill when she calls to me again.

"Okay, well? We're about to close?"

"Yeah," I say, fingering the rhinestone buckles. Just a minute.

I'd forgotten how heavy the material was. All the lining underneath.

Slipping it over my head, I'm temporarily blinded. And when I come out of the wide neckhole, I'm still blinded. The track lights, I realize, have gone off above my head. The muzak has abruptly ceased, cutting off Michael Bolton in mid-croon. They're getting serious.

They knock and knock and the dress hangs heavy on me in

the dark. They call, ma'am, ma'am, and I'd say something, but I'm voiceless. Because I thought for sure I'd be swimming in it. Drowning in it, even. That the space between where I ended and the dress began would be miles and miles and miles. But even in the dark, I feel how it's closer than I thought. Dangerously close. And if I wait until my eyes adjust, I'll be able to maybe make out my silhouette in the mirror, I'll be able to measure how much.

Beyond the Sea

Living in the South Tower of Phase One in the Beyond the Sea complex, my bedroom window overlooks the Malibu Club Spa and Fitness Centre, which means the first thing I see when I wake up each morning is my neighbor Char's triumph over the ineptitudes of the flesh. Depending on how many times I hit snooze, I'll see her doing leg lifts or thigh abductions or this weird hip jiggle move where she'll stand in front of the mirror, put her hands on her protruding hip bones, and wiggle from side to side in a way that, even though I'm barely awake, profoundly embarrasses me. Most of the time, though, my eyes will open to the sight of her hunched over Lifecycle One, literally all of her bones from the waist up draped over the handlebars in submission to The Task, which, I can only assume, from this vantage point, is the obliteration of the Body Mass Index.

After I wake, I'll stand there looking down at her from the window a long time, even though it exhausts me—physically, spiritually—to watch her. Oddly, from this distance, I find I feel no hatred even though she is my sworn enemy, even though I know a showdown regarding the time slot issue is inevitable. Sometimes a pity will even bloom in my heart for that small, hunched, pedaling figure. But not for long. Looking down upon her from six floors up, I enjoy a moment of something close to clarity before I shrug on my gym clothes and prepare to dethrone her.

As I make my way to the Malibu Club, which sits between Phase One and Phase Two of Beyond the Sea, a gated community that has nothing to do with California (we are nowhere near California), I brace myself for the inevitable confrontation. I enter the gym, which smells, as it always does, of stale sweat and rancid mop fronds, and eye the Cardio Equipment Booking Sheet, where I've purposefully printed my name for the 7:00 to 7:30 slot for Lifecycle One in big block letters, pressing deep into the page. I see her name sitting above mine in cursive for the 6:30 to 7:00 slot. Mine in unsharpened pencil. Hers in irrefutable ink. Though her handwriting seems easy breezy, I'm not fooled by those lackadaisical loops. I know from experience that she will not go gently into the time slot change.

I'm right. Though it's seven a.m. on the dot by the gym clock and 7:02 by my own watch, which has been set according to the world clock, she's still on the Lifecycle, pedaling like she isn't cooling down anytime soon. Thus far, I have chosen to be the bigger person. First, I do some passive-aggressive calf stretching within her peripheral vision. When she still grips those handlebars like she'll never relinquish them, I stand closer beside her, doing shoulder circles while burning holes into the side of her face with my eyes. When still she proves impervious, I ahem.

She turns to look at me and it is terrifying, this moment

when I am forced to take in the whole of her cardiovascular effort from up close. The sweat rivulets dribbling down the hollows of her haphazardly made-up face. Those blotches of coral blush she burns into each cheek. On her pursed mouth, a slash of lipstick the color of blanched tangerines. The way she looks at me, eyes wide and full of a cardio-induced fury, makes me feel the pouchiness of my lower abdomen, the cumbersome fact of my thigh flesh sticking together, the batwings that Harold told me would take time, to be patient (he once had a client on whom they just suddenly disappeared one day like magic, he says). She's taking it all in, my whole fat-to-muscle ratio, and I know it's making me less credible in her eyes, which say she has named me. Probably something like Inconsistent Gym User. Or Fat Ass.

"Are you on here next?" she asks me. As if she didn't already know that in her soy milk–fed soul.

"Yes," I say, like it's news to both of us. Unfortunate news that I'm sorry to be the bearer of. Like it's going to rain frogs today, I'm afraid. Storm them. So sorry.

She looks from me to the clock and shakes her head like we are both her enemy. Like the clock and I are in cahoots. According to Ruth, she's written notes to management about that clock on the Comment Sheet, complaining that it is three minutes fast.

Seeing that time is against her, she returns her gaze to the swimming pool, where the Aquafit women are bobbing up and down in unison to the sound of "Kokomo," their fleshy bodies making the green water waggle. Though her nod, barely perceptible, tells me she has registered this terrible knowledge about her time being up, she doesn't get off. In fact, for a few minutes, she actually grips the handlebars tighter and pedals faster, forcing me to contemplate her long, fibrous mass of back and recall how many minutes she's stolen from me over the past two years. They add up. Like anything else. Those sticks of Trident I don't chew. Those tamari toasted almonds and crystalized ginger hunks I try not to steal from the Bulk Barn. That handful of microwaved Orville I do my best to refuse from my father on a Friday night during a *Fawlty Towers* marathon, a regular occurrence now that I have moved back east. I draw in breath to ahem once more but she beats me to it, getting off the machine in a sudden huff. Tugs hard on the paper towel dispenser. Sprays the machine with disinfectant. Wipes it down improperly. Then storms off toward the stretching mats to begin her long and complex toning routine. Making me feel, you know, like *I'm* the small, petty one.

By the time she gets off the Lifecycle and I get on, I've only got twenty-four minutes left, by the gym clock, before the anorexic flight attendant shows up with her sinew and her Spanish fashion magazines and begins anxiously shifting her birdlike weight from right to left behind me. I do my best to make these minutes count but it isn't easy. I can't help but feel like this time slot, so hard-won, isn't making much of a dent. Harold says I ought to Trust the Process, Love the Journey. He's here at Malibu now, standing over one of his oldest clients, Margo, whose body, as long as I have known her, has resembled a potato perched on two toothpicks. He's got Margo balanced on a BOSU ball and, though she's teetering violently, he's encouraging her to do one-legged squats. Margo's a fighter, though. She's flailing, chin up. I catch Harold's eye in the mirror and he mouths, Monday, at me over Margo's shaking limbs. Then he punches the air a little and winks.

On either side of me, I feel how the other 7:00 a.m. time slot people are already minutes into their rowing and treading and cycling and ellipticaling. Mainly women of a certain age. I try not to look at them. If I look at their temple sweat, at their mouths half-open and panting, at their faces contorted with focus or thought annihilation or dreams of impossible future selves, at their eyes skimming pulp fiction or fashion magazines, at their leg cellulite, which is just as discernible through their gym shorts as it was when I first moved here two years ago, I'll begin to feel like we're all a bunch of sad, fat Rodentia upon whom a terrible, sick joke is being played. Like somewhere up there in the cheap stucco ceiling is a hidden camera and an audience laughing uproariously at our useless sweat beads, our mottled flesh, which these hours have done nothing to excise.

Instead, I keep my gaze fixed straight ahead into the floor-to-ceiling windows, which look right into the swimming pool, and I watch the arm flapping of the Aquafit women. They remind me of this bird I once saw in a nature film who was trying to escape an oil spill. It was awful to watch those wings flap uselessly, to witness the inevitable triumph of the dark oil. Yet I couldn't help but bear witness, then and now. There is something about their department store swimwear, their grim sloshing, which is as hypnotic to me as undulating jellyfish. Some young unfortunate woman in denim shorts stands at the pool's edge, doing the motions in the air that their iceberg-like bodies are all meant to parrot underwater. She must be their new teacher. In my many, albeit intermittent, sessions in the 7:00 a.m. time slot, I have witnessed the Aquafit women terrorize their way through three. No one looks especially pleased to be following this new girl either, except for one man, a Russian eccentric whom I often see in the evenings, sifting through the recycling bins looking for I'm not sure what. Because of his big enthusiastic splashes, the women give him a wide berth. I think they suspect him of mocking them and would try to have him banned, except that they also fear him slightly.

"It's *your* time and you have to make that clear," Ruth tells me later that night over Iron Maidens and Warrior Bowls at Zen, an eatery conveniently located within the Beyond the Sea complex. Ruth's a divorce lawyer and Treadmill Three enthusiast who lives on the top floor in Phase Two. She didn't handle my divorce, but she did give me lots of free advice. Being a treadmill user, she doesn't have to deal with Char, though as a Malibu Club veteran, she's well aware of her and is sympathetic to the time slot issue.

"You have to be firm," Ruth says, pointing her chopsticks at me. It's the kind of place that gives you chopsticks with your meal even though you're eating salad. To make it fun. "It's not as if you can reason with her. She won't listen to reason."

"Where is she getting these pens to write her name down is what I want to know," I say. "I never see anything but pencils on that Cardio Booking Sheet podium."

Ruth hunts through her baby kale for hidden hearts of palm. "Didn't you know? She brings down her own."

"You're not serious."

She nods, sips her Iron Maiden, and makes a face at the taste. It looks like black sludge but supposedly it's good for the blood—for energy, which we need. "I've seen her do it. Tucks it in her bike shorts."

"But that's insane. Why would someone do that?"

"Isn't it obvious? She's terrified someone is going to erase her name."

"But that's ridiculous. Those podium pencils don't even have erasers," I point out.

"We're not exactly dealing with a rational being here," Ruth says, readjusting her black shrug, worn, on this hot day, presumably to conceal her upper arm flesh.

"How sad," I say. "What a sad existence."

"Of course it's sad. It's terribly sad." As she digs into her greens with her chopsticks, I watch the flesh near her armpit, the part not covered by the shrug, swing slightly in her zeal.

"I guess I could just switch to Lifecycle Three," I say. "Have done with her altogether."

"Why should *you* have to make adjustments?" Ruth says. "Besides," she adds, "you hate Lifecycle Three. Didn't you tell me once being on it was like being in a nightmare?"

"Yeah," I say. It really is. The handlebars aren't quite in sync with the pedals. Ruth said she'd try to bring that up at the next condo board member meeting. Ruth's on the board.

"So why even consider it? It's like me with Treadmill Three. I don't know why but it works for me. You have to go with what *works* for you, you know?"

I nod, looking through the glass-top table at Ruth's stomach, which, despite her unwavering dedication to the Malibu Club and the fact that two of her dinners are delivered to her door each week by Hearthealth, has not diminished in all the time I've known her. In fact, Ruth basically looks like a slightly deflated version of the pretty seventeen-year-old fat girl she showed me a picture of when I went to her place once. This picture, displayed on the mantel of her fake fireplace, is meant to bolster her spirits, remind her how far she has come.

She asks me if I know Christine, from Phase Two.

"Christine?"

"She might have been before your time," Ruth says with a dismissive wave of a hand. "Anyway, Christine had that 7:00 a.m. slot for ages. Had the same problem. With Char. The two of them even had it out in the gym once. Christine was firm with her, though. She told Char in no uncertain terms that she was impinging on her time slot."

"What happened?"

"Char threw a fit. Of course. It was ugly. But she got off in the end. She had no choice. I told you, you have to be firm with her. You have to put her in her place."

I picture putting Char in her place. What that would entail. Her frantic pedaling. Me prying her off the handlebars bone by bone.

"I don't know. I feel bad about it, though. I do. It all feels so . . . petty."

Ruth looks at me for a moment, then sets down her chopsticks.

"Remember that period you went through a little while ago when you were signing your name up for cardio machines but then not showing up in the morning?"

I color when Ruth says this. "Yeah."

"Well," Ruth says, leaning in, "*she* was the one writing NO SHOW beside your name."

"She didn't!"

"She did."

I remember those terrible block letters. Underlined three times. Surrounded by exclamations. That accusing arrow pointing to my scrawled name. I remember thinking, Who in their right mind would do such a thing? I remember now they were in ink.

"Jesus. Who does that?"

"Of course," Ruth says, "she didn't act alone. She *was* spurred on by certain parties. After all, she's got her allies too."

"But that's ridiculous," I say. "How did my not showing up inconvenience her? Or anyone? Anyone can claim the machine after the five-minute default period." It's true. That anyone can do so is a well-placarded rule.

Ruth picks at the dregs of her Warrior Bowl and says nothing. I remember that people signing up for machines and then not showing up is a serious pet peeve of hers too. It's awkward, this moment. Despite having known each other for two years, we're not that close.

"I'm angry now," I say.

"You should be. I would be."

"That's just so . . . sick. She's *sick*."

We discuss how sick she is, a favorite topic. How her bones have grown more visible lately. How her T-shirts hang on her like oversize sacks with armholes.

"What does she even eat, do you think?"

"Tea fungus," Ruth says. "Unsweetened. From an eyedropper. Is what I picture. Either that or some sort of sea vegetable."

"Sad," I say.

"It is," Ruth muses.

We decide to order two skim milk cappuccinos and split a gluten-free carrot cake cupcake.

"Do you think that scale in the Malibu Club is accurate?" I ask, watching Ruth saw the cupcake in two with a chopstick.

"I think so. I don't know. It might be a bit wonky. Why?"

"Oh, just lately I've been weighing myself every day on it and that number just won't budge. It's, like, stuck. Or something. Do you find that too? That it's stuck?"

Ruth assesses the cupcake halves to make certain they're even, then hands me my half. I stare at it, think of the treat dinners I used to have with Tom. We'd go for ice cream and he would always eat his very slowly, so that after I'd inhaled mine and was sad that it was gone, he could pass me his unfinished bowl. *I can't eat all that,* I'd say. *Sure you can,* he'd say without looking at me because he knew that if he looked at me I wouldn't take it. *Take it. You deserve it. It's your night off. Anyway, you know I don't care about this stuff.* I took it, feeling bad about myself because I couldn't resist it. I hated feeling like even after all the positive changes I'd made, I wasn't above this need and he was. I resented him for it, even though I knew that all there was behind his gesture was kindness. Love for me that made him look away while I ate.

We still send each other songs sometimes. Mostly he'll send them to me. New songs by old bands we loved. New songs by new bands he thinks I might love now. Most of the time, I can't listen to them. Sometimes I'll listen to them and a wave in me will break briefly and then I'll have to turn it off.

"I used to weigh myself every day but these days I'm trying to get away from the scale," Ruth says. "I'm through attaching myself to a certain number, you know? I find I'm healthier that way, mentally speaking."

"Right," I say.

I watch her take tiny bites of her cupcake half to make it last.

After each bite, she raises her eyebrows and nods like she is receiving surprising but not unwelcome news. She does look healthy. Her skin glows and her hair shines and she seems genuinely content.

"You know when you're on Treadmill Three? Do you ever feel like a gerbil?"

Ruth frowns, licks a bit of icing from the corner of her mouth. "A *gerbil*?"

"Any rodent, really. You know, on a wheel? You know," I continue. "Sort of like the joke's on us?"

She sits back in her chair, making it squeak. She stares at me for a moment. "The joke's on us? What do you mean?"

"Well, you know how some people? They go to the gym regularly and they don't look any different? Like, at all?" When I say this, I feel her gaze flit over my frame.

"And it's like, all that time, all that energy, you know? When we could have been . . ."

"When we could have been . . ." Ruth prompts me, impatient.

I have an image of something like Paris. Some woman walking for the sake of walking. With actual friends. She's happy.

"I don't know. Something."

She shrugs.

"I don't know what you're driving at, exactly, but I *will* say this: On the days that I don't work out? I, for one, definitely *feel* a difference. Yes. Without a doubt."

She takes a sip of her stevia-sweetened skim milk cappuccino as if to seal this statement. Then consults her watch. She says speaking of which, she's only ten hours away from her next time slot. We'd better get the check.

I want to grab her by her shrug lapels and confess that I'm an unbeliever. That being on that machine makes me feel like I'm running in some sucking substance worse than mud. I can find no foothold, no traction. That I feel out of control, inches from the lip of the abyss. That while we've been sitting here, there's this angry, hungry maw in me that is fathoms deep. But even though Ruth's only a hair thinner than I am, she's way on the other side of the fat girl spectrum, looking at me from the safe, slightly smug distance of her own control and conviction.

So I say, "I know what you mean. Me too. Absolutely."

As we leave Zen, making our way to our respective Phases, I call out to her, "Hey. So whatever happened to Christine? The woman with the 7:00 a.m. time slot? She move?"

"No, she's still here. Moved to Phase Three now, I think. But she doesn't come to the Club anymore. Sort of fell off the wagon. See you tomorrow?" she calls out to me, with her key fob already out.

"I'll be there with bells on," I say.

On the elevator ride back up to my apartment, I can already feel the cupcake half doing its worst and I think of how many Lifecycle minutes it will take to atone. More minutes than she will ever be willing to part with.

When the elevator door opens on my floor, I see a striped British shorthair, one of Char's, dart past me. She'll do this. Let them roam the corridors in the evening. She calls it "airing" them.

I've learned a bit about her cats via clipped conversations in the elevator, though we'll always avoid a ride together if we can help it. I know one is asthmatic and one is prone to seizures, but I forget which requires needles and which needs a pill that Char has to crush and mix in with its food. I'm sympathetic, having recently parted with an injection-dependent cat of my own, Mr. Benchley. When I adopted him, shortly after I left Tom, he was already sick and old.

In the corridor, I crouch down beside the cat, hold out my hand for her to sniff. She sniffs but keeps her distance. Behind me I feel the door to Char's apartment open. I know she's standing in the doorframe watching me but I don't look at her. Instead, I ask the cat, "What's your name?"

"Toffee," Char says behind me. "After her coat."

"Well, Toffee," I say. "You're beautiful. You are. You are you are you are."

Then I get up, swaying a bit before I catch my balance, and stagger toward my front door without once looking back, without saying good night.

When I stumble into my own apartment, I am stabbed in the thigh by the sharp edge of my mother's glass credenza, which, after she died, I couldn't bring myself to throw away.

I do not like to think, as I lie here, already dreading tomorrow morning's rigors, feeling myself swell from Zen and hating Ruth for it, about how Char and I share a bedroom wall. I lean against the eggshell primer I know she is likely leaning on the other side of. Is she consuming fermented sea kelp from an eyedropper? Gloating over the protrusion of her spine nodules? Tallying up her visible ribs with an abacus? Sometimes I'll lean there and listen in for evidence of a secret life. How I would love for her to have a secret life. What I hear is disappointing. What I hear is silence. A sitcom with a laugh track. Could be *Frasier*. The opening and closing of a closet door.

The next morning, I finally have it out with her. I feel it in the air all the way to the Malibu Club that today will be the day of our inevitable confrontation. Finding her still bone-flogging the Life-cycle when I come into the gym at 7:00:00, I stride right up to her and I ahem. And when she turns her awful sweaty visage toward me, I do not clam up, I do not cower. I tell her point-blank that I am on this machine next, as she well knows. And when she says, "Just give me a few minutes," like I'm a fly that just needs to be swatted, I remind her, loudly, within earshot of every ineffectually working-out woman, that she cut into my time yesterday and the day before that and the day before that, and that's when she cuts me off and shouts, "Fine! Fine! Fine! *Relax!*" And though a red fog burns the back of my neck, I do not waver. I remain standing there, my arms folded over my faded JUST DO IT T-shirt, silently supervising her cleaning of the seat and handlebars. I even point out the splotches of skull sweat she missed on the pedal straps. When I do this, I think she's going to smack me, but she just turns away and wipes those down too. When she's finished, she runs toward the stretching mats, swearing, and I hear, under her breath, her name for me. It is worse than mine for her. It is worse than any name I have ever hurled at myself in the mirror like a rock. It is worse than anything I could have ever imagined.

To work out in the wake of her all, the humid wake of her all, is always a disorienting experience. Today, it is like working out in the aftermath of a war, like treading bone- and blood- and skull-strewn earth. The handlebars are still poker hot from where she gripped them, seemingly for dear life. The monitor is still damp from her hasty wipe down. Her sweat splotches still ghost the pedal straps.

And from the corner I feel the pointed blade of her anger aimed at the back of my neck as she matrix-lunges, as she farmer-walks and hip-wiggles and abducts. One angry, pared-down leg, then the other. As I mount the still-smoking machine, I feel the truth of what her outraged eyes are etching into my back, that these minutes will make no difference to what Harold delicately refers to as my problem areas. Then I see Ruth mouth, Good for you, and nod from where she is doing isometric shoulder holds in the mirror. And I propel one ludicrous foot in front of the other, even though it's like that nightmare where I'm running on terribly soft earth, running even as the ground gives way beneath me.

To distract myself, I watch the Aquafit women, who, I observe, once more have no teacher. One of the class members is leading them now. I watch them go through the motions of their absurd water dance, knowing they are doomed to inhabit their masses of hanging flesh forever.

And it's too much. I get off. I get off three minutes earlier than my time. I expect Char to chide me for this with her eyes but when I turn to look at the mats, I see she's gone. No trace of her but a dent in the mat, speckled with a few of her sweat driblets. I wipe the machine down for the hungry-looking flight attendant, who has been behind me all this time, circling inside my field of vision, pointedly stretching. Seeing me get off early, she gives me a skull-like grin in gratitude. What a boon, these extra minutes, her eyes say. I can feel her patting herself on her shoulder tendons for all those days when she came in earlier, in the name of *You never know.* *Maybe the fat girl will finally throw in the towel, give up.* Well, that day has come. All yours, I tell her. And watching her gleefully tether the ropes of herself to the machine makes me so exhausted, I do not

even do my post-cardio cobra. Or plank. Or those leg lifts and scis-
sor kicks and thigh abductions that I'm fairly certain do not work
anyway. It is all, I am convinced now, a terrible trick.

I do not go to the gym the next morning. Or the next. Or the next.
In short, I relinquish my precarious grip on the 7:00 a.m. time
slot. I give in to the abyss. There follows another bout of darkness,
in which nothing is measured or counted or weighed, in which I
dress before the mirror not seeing myself. A period during which
the Malibu Club, observed from six floors up, becomes a strange
and distant aquarium full of curious fish and Char its saddest
specimen. I watch her each morning from above, glutted on my
abdicated minutes, and under my breath, I say, You win. Happy?
But she does not look happy. She looks as angry as ever.

    Evenings, I eat large quantities of the Foods I Should Avoid
with my father. We have an unspoken agreement that if he doesn't
mention Tom, my divorce, my mother, or how I currently live,
then he can come over from time to time and we can sit on opposite ends of my mother's white couch with the pale blue flowers
on it and watch *Absolutely Fabulous*. In this way, we've gradually
grown closer in the years since I moved back home.

    "Friday night," my father says, turning to me. "No plans?"

    "No."

    "Don't you have a friend who lives nearby? The old one.
What's her name? Mal?"

    "Mel." Mel lives in a condo complex just east and north of
here. It has a name too. Eden. East of Eden. Something like that.

    "So?"

    "We see each other sometimes." That used to be true, but
now we haven't in more than a year. For a while after I moved

back, we'd meet up every few months or so for coffee or a drink in the afternoon. Have a stilted conversation about her boyfriend, whether I was dating anyone, her work, my work, for about two hours, then one of us, usually Mel, would bring up all the things we had to do the next day. Better be heading off. But it was good to see you. It was good to see you too. We should do it more often. We should. We've grown apart, I guess. Some friends do.

Tonight, I can feel him wanting to ask me more questions but he doesn't. Instead he hands me a bowl of microwaved Orville Redenbacher's. Tonight, I do not refuse him. I accept. And after the popcorn is polished off, then, together, we eat a box of stale brandy-filled chocolate beans.

When he gets up to get himself a glass of water, he hits his head on my mother's low-hanging iron candelabra. This often happens. As always, he sighs a little but says nothing.

When I first moved back here from out west, he used to tell me I should get rid of my mother's stuff. Then he would ask me if I ever thought of getting rid of it. Now he just sits on it and says nothing. Props his feet on the sharp-edged glass-and-chrome surfaces. Sometimes I'll see him looking over at my mother's ashes on the mantel of my fake fireplace. Housed in an undusted blue urn patterned with big, tacky flowers. The pattern reminded me of the one you find on muumuus or the sorts of clothes they used to sell in fat-girl stores, the kind my mother wore all of her adult life, the kind I wore for a large chunk of my youth, the kind fat girls and women had to wear before everyone got fat, before supply met demand. Perhaps there were more options urn-wise beyond the muumuu one, but at the time, in my grief, I didn't see them. And anyway, I told myself at the time, she wouldn't be in there long. I'd release her soon. Scatter her into a body of water, which is what she told me she wanted. Now, years later, I keep thinking I'll do this, have even pictured myself at the edge of how many expanses of gray, lapping water, or sometimes it's a river, the water dark and moving quickly, too quickly, or sometimes it's a blue-green expanse and very still. I'm wearing a long dark gray coat. I'm right on the rocky shore. I'm right at the edge of the long pier. I'm right on the stony riverbank. I'm leaning over the bridge rail. I'm standing with my feet in the white wet sand that is the shore of this green waving sea that will house my mother. The muumuu urn is heavy in my hands. But no matter how many bodies of water I have stood over in my mind, no body seems right. Certainly not that lake I see a sliver of through my window. Or whatever it is. What is it? A reservoir. A man-made expanse of wet. Not the sea, surely.

"That lake goes out to sea, right?" I ask my father.

"To the sea?" he repeats, his eyes on the TV. "I'm sure it does. It has to, doesn't it?"

When my father gets up to leave, he hits his head again on the candelabra and swears.

"Do you ever light this or . . . ?"

"Sometimes."

"You should light it. If you're going to keep it, you should light it." My father is currently seeing two different women in the building, both of whom live in Phase One, both on the fifth floor but in different towers. Both are efficient, evening gym users, one slightly more so than the other. When he's finished hanging out with me, he will go back up to see her.

"Good night," I tell him.

After he leaves, I go to bed, and I dream the recurring dream in which I blow up Bebe, the women's clothing store. When the smurf salesgirl tells me she doesn't have the peacock blazer I want in a medium, even though I am not a medium, I am a tenuous, hard-won large, I tell her it's fine. And it is, for once. Because I can feel the dynamite strapped to my stomach under my XL Ann Taylor cardigan. When I show her why it's fine, she screams and I scream and then up we all go in smoke. The strappy bodycons. The billowy, asymmetrical blouses. The whole of their rhinestone-studded aerobic line. And even though I die in the great fire, I also get to watch it burn from above. And it's beautiful to behold the mushroom cloud, the bauble ash, to feel the hot wind of the explosion in my hair. But the sirens and alarms that signal Bebe's end are beyond the dream too, they are in my apartment, they are deafening. I open my eyes. Fire alarm. The voice of Carlos, the night security person, telling us, Do not panic, Do not panic, over the PA system that is piped into every unit.

I shrug on a housecoat and stumble out. I stagger toward the emergency exit, passing by Char's apartment as I do. Her door is wide open.

From the doorframe, I watch her pace a flipped-over version of my own floor plan. She's got one cat tucked under her arm, and she's calling out "Toffee!" in a shrill voice. She's still in her workout T-shirt. Jogging pants that hang on her. And over that, an open ratty robe. As I watch her, I think of the one-eyed tiger I saw at a zoo once. How she walked back and forth across the length of her stone enclosure while we all watched. I stood there with my head against the glass, feeling her panic and misery in my bones for I don't know how long, until a child beside me piped up, *Why is she pacing like that?*

She's tense, the zookeeper said.

And I remember hatching a plan to free her then and there. I'd come back at night. Hop the spiked fence. Hurl a garbage can at the hand-thumped glass. Ride the tiger into the night if she didn't eat me first.

As I enter her apartment, my peripheral vision registers the absence of food on the granite kitchen counters, the tall vases of blown glass brimming with fake orchids, the sleek tables and chairs, the amorphous metallic statues. Details I will store to tell Ruth later over Iron Maidens.

Can you believe how she lives?
It's sad.
It is sad.
What a sad existence.

Though she doesn't ask for help and I don't offer, I follow her into her living room. We both crouch down on her eggshell carpet (I see that she too opted for eggshell over taupe). There, under the wicker love seat, right beneath its sagging underbelly, I see a couple of yellow eyes wide open. Toffee.

Char lifts one end of the love seat while I attempt to gather Toffee, hissing and spitting, into my arms. To do this, I have to pry her paws from the carpet claw by claw. I carry her with her legs straight out and her claws unsheathed and aimed at my neck, all the way out of the apartment and down the concrete stairs toward the ground floor emergency exit. We leave the building, walk toward the grassy verge between the parking lot and the Malibu Club, where the sound of the alarm is slightly fainter.

We sit on the overclipped, parched grass, between crop circles of bland landscaping. Flowers planted like sentinels, flowers so boring they have no names. The cats hiss in our arms. We do not speak or look at one another. Above us, the pink blaze of the morning begins to rim the night. She does not thank me. When I look at her, I see she is looking straight ahead into the aquarium windows of the Malibu Club. She's watching a woman there, on Lifecycle One, pedaling in the dark. I do that sometimes, if I can't sleep. I'll come down early, before the real estate agents and business analysts start arriving for the 5:30 a.m. time slot. I'll keep the lights off until some asshole in a terry cloth headband comes down and flips a switch. Somehow it's easier to pedal in the dark, to put one ridiculous, unbelieving foot in front of the other with just the exit signs and the blinking red lights of the cardio machines to contend with.

I've seen the pedaling woman there before. Apart from the Aquafit diehards, you cannot imagine a creature more stagnant in terms of results. She's like a soap opera that you tune in to after ten years only to find that the plot hasn't moved an inch. All the love triangles and intrigues and scandals are exactly where you last left them. The actors are just a bit older, on their faces more evidence of cosmetic preservation.

"Haven't seen you down there lately," Char says, jutting her chin toward the dark windows of the club.

"No," I say.

"Taking a break?"

"Sort of."

She nods sagely and reaches into the pocket of her robe for a pack of cigarettes. She extends the pack toward me like a question. I shake my head.

"Do you like the zoo much?" she asks me, lighting one.

"The zoo? Yes. Sometimes."

"I work there, you know. Fund-raising."

"Do you?" I say, like I don't already know this.

"I could get you a couple free passes," she says. "You know, for you and a friend."

I think of Mel. How when we were in high school, we used to go to the zoo and she'd bring me into the monkey room just because she knew I was terrified of them, and then, feeling guilty, she'd lead me away toward the turtles. Looking back, it still doesn't add up how we went from lying in the grass and listening to the same set of headphones to where we are now. Nowhere. I really need to e-mail her.

"I might even be able to arrange a behind-the-scenes tour. Not of every animal, obviously. But one, maybe. Your favorite."

Silence.

"So what's your favorite?"

"I don't know. Turtle?" I tell her.

"Turtle," she repeats. I can tell my choice disappoints her. I should have chosen some breed of big cat. A cheetah. A lynx.

"Shouldn't be too difficult. Just give me notice. I'll need notice," she says. "To make arrangements."

I nod and watch this woman pedaling in the dark. Was I like her? Surely not. Surely I was getting somewhere. Surely all my work was the work of progress toward attainable goals.

"Sad," Char pipes up beside me. I see she's looking at the woman too.

"Yes," I agree. "Very sad."

The cat's grip on my arm relinquishes a little.

"If she would just do interval training. That's her problem. No interval training."

Smoke darts out of her mouth like little tongues.

"Your body needs to be surprised. Attacked. Always. You've

got to shock your system constantly. Otherwise, you're no-where."

"Yeah," I say, looking at the woman. "Do you know if this lake goes out to the sea?"

"The sea? I don't think so."

I nod.

"Maybe eventually it does," she says. "I think it goes into a river first. I'm not sure."

I wonder where it all goes, Mel asked me once.

What?

Our fat. After we lose it. I know we sweat but that can't be all it is. It can't just turn into water and salt. It can't just disappear. We don't just melt, do we?

She looked at me, smiling, bouncing a little in her chair. She was in a good mood because she'd been on a diet for a while, was losing. Feeling philosophical in her slinky velvet dress, stirring a peppermint tea she'd doctored with a million Twins.

I think we do melt, actually, I told her. *I read an article about it once in a science magazine. I can't remember exactly what it said, though. I think it even comes out in our breath.*

Mel wasn't listening. She was looking at her reflection in the window, pleased.

Maybe it's all around us, she said at last, waving a hand at the dusty café air, making her voice spooky, her eyes big and wide like we were teenagers and she was trying to scare me. *Maybe we're all around us. Maybe the universe is made up of it. Our old fat.* She smiled. *Wouldn't that be so funny?*

The red fire of the morning is ablaze over our faces and over the water. The glass towers of the city, which will return to a dismal gray the moment the sun is done rising, shimmer and flame in the distance. From here the lake looks beautiful, but I know for a fact, have seen with my own eyes during the walks I sometimes take to mix it up, that nothing lives under there but the junk of the world and eyeless, acid-ridden fish. I suppose I could switch to a different machine. Vary the incline level at two-minute intervals. Change the fitness course constantly so that I'm always going from Random to Fat Burning to Rolling Hills, so that it always feels like I'm getting somewhere. The sound of the sirens draws close, causing Char's cat to tense in my arms. Even though I know that woman must hear the sirens through the glass enclosure of the Malibu Club, she keeps pedaling. As I watch her through the glass, breathing in Char's smoke, I feel dangerously close to a knowledge that is probably already ours for the taking, a knowledge that I know could change everything.

ACKNOWLEDGMENTS

Thank you to my parents, Nina Milosevic and James Awad, for their love and faith in me.

Thank you to Alexandra Dimou, Ken Calhoun, Jessica Riley, Jennifer Long-Pratt, Erica Mena-Landry, Dawn Promislow, Mairead Case, and Emily Cullitone for their friendship, immense support, kindness, and thoughtful feedback during the writing of this book.

Thank you to Jessica Riley, an intelligent and beyond generous reader whose friendship and endless encouragement saved me more times than I can say, for my sanity.

Thank you to my inspiring teacher Brian Evenson for his perceptive and encouraging feedback, and for the invaluable guidance provided by Joanna Howard, Carole Maso, Thalia Field, Joanna Ruocco, and Kate Bernheimer as well as my fantastic cohort at Brown (2012–2014) who patiently read various incarnations of this book.

Thank you to the generous editors who read and supported

my writing: Nick Mount, Jordan Bass, Derek Webster, Matthew Fox, Carmine Starnino, Jaime Clarke, and Mary Cotton at Newtonville Books, Libby Hodges, Mikhail Iossel, Mike Spry, Emma Komlos-Hrobsky, Emily M. Keeler, Lauren Spohrer, Quinn Emmett, and Elizabeth Blachman. Thank you to Christine Vines.

Thank you to my amazing, hardworking agent Julia Kenny, whose enthusiasm is a bright light in my moments of doubt and to my editor, Lindsey Schwoeri, for her always intelligent and insightful feedback and her tireless dedication to this book. Her commitment to authenticity and voice was yet more proof that I couldn't have had a better editor. And many thanks too to my Canadian editor Nicole Winstanley, for her thoughtful notes, her deep commitment to this book, and for bringing it to my home and native land.

Thank you to Debka Colson and the Writers' Room of Boston for providing space in which to work.

Thank you to Betsy Burton for opening her home and giving me space and time to write and to everyone at The King's English bookshop for their friendship and community and for giving me a job when I needed one.

Lastly, my deepest thanks to Rex Baker, to whom this book is dedicated, and whose belief and love saw me through everything. I could not have written this without you.